THE NEWCASTLE FORGOTTEN FANTASY LIBRARY
VOLUME XII

CHILD CHRISTOPHER AND GOLDILIND THE FAIR

CHILD CHRISTOPHER
AND GOLDILIND
THE FAIR

BY

WILLIAM MORRIS

NEWCASTLE PUBLISHING COMPANY, INC.
NORTH HOLLYWOOD, CALIFORNIA
1977

A NEWCASTLE BOOK
FIRST PRINTING APRIL 1977
PRINTED IN THE UNITED STATES OF AMERICA

NOTE

OF this original romance but one edition was ever issued by its author.[1] It is thus described in *A Note by William Morris on His Aims in Founding the Kelmscott Press: Together with a Short Description of the Press by S. C. Cockerell and an Annotated List of the Books printed thereat* (MDCCCXCVIII):

CHILD CHRISTOPHER AND GOLDILIND THE FAIR. BY WILLIAM MORRIS. 2 vols. 16mo. Chaucer type. In black and red. Borders 15a and 15, and woodcut title. 600 on paper at fifteen shillings, 12 on vellum at four guineas. Dated July 25, issued September 25, 1895. Published by William Morris. Bound in half holland, with labels printed in the Golden type.

The borders designed for this book were only used once again, in Hand and Soul. The plot of

---

[1] "In the summer of 1895 he issued from his press a delightful prose romance which he had originally begun to write in four-foot trochaic couplets, but had desisted before completing the seventeenth line." (*The Books of William Morris. By H. Buxton Forman.* London, 1897.)

the story was suggested by that of Havelok the Dane, printed by the Early English Text Society.

At the Edelheim sale (March 7th, 1900), a copy brought $35.00, and at still later sales it has realized from $26.00 to $34.00.

CONTENTS

CONTENTS

INTRODUCTION

You are about to read a comfortably familiar, startlingly new story. It is a story as old as English literature and as contemporary as the latest best-seller. It manages to achieve remarkable forward and backward movements through time because it inhabits the transcendent world of the imagination. And you are among the very select few who have ever had a chance to glimpse this delicate and perceptive vision. Until this Newcastle Forgotten Fantasy edition, in the eighty-odd years since it was written, *Child Christopher and Goldilind the Fair* has existed in only about 2,000 copies, scattered in various small editions around the world. Though it has been little known, the book is intriguing and important. It provides access to the literary and mythic roots of fantasy writing; it shows us, more simply and directly than any of his other novels, the influences and ideals which led its author, William Morris, to discover a new mode of fiction.

William Morris illuminates the nineteenth century as the man who created the English fantasy novel. In doing so he transformed the older forms of literature he most admired—epic, romance, saga, and folk-tale—into the widely read format of novelistic fiction. Morris radically departed from the conventions of social and psychological realism which dominated the mainstream Victorian novel. His first major biographer, J. W. Mackail, accurately observed in 1899 that "On the imaginative side he was far behind, and far before, his own time: he belongs partly to the earlier Middle Ages, and partly to an age still far in the future." We are now far enough into that future to begin to recognize the magnitude of his literary invention. He appreciated and created a literature which revealed itself in action rather than introspection, and one in which symbols were vital parts of the action and setting, not artificially contrived literary devices. He wrote of a nobler and better world, hoping to appeal to the highest motives of men to live honest, decent lives in a climate of fair politics and good government. These humanitarian visions he combined with myth and symbol into active narration, a technique he adapted from epic, saga, and romance writing.

Morris was a man of enormous energy and wide learning. His poetic achievement earned him the offer of the poet laureateship of England after Tennyson's death, but he declined it because of other priorities. His artistic range extended from the mastery of dozens of design and craft skills to that of scholar and translator of *Beowulf, The Aeneid, The Odyssey,* and the great Norse epics. In the preface to his first translations for the six-volume Saga Library, Morris praised the fact that Iceland "retained the memory of the mythology and the hero-tales of the Gothic tribes . . . the poetic life and instinct which made Iceland the treasure-house of the mythology of the whole Teutonic race." His scholarly and literary sensibilities merged with social criticism: he felt called upon to praise and preserve this "treasure-house" because it represented a collection of ancient stories saved through precarious oral traditions over hundreds of years.

Describing himself late in life, Morris observed that "Apart from the desire to produce beautiful things, the leading passion of my life has been and is hatred of modern civilization." By this he indicated that he discerned a ruinous tendency in his generation's preoccupation with becoming self-consciously "modern." Imaginatively, linguistically, culturally and historically, human life began to cut itself off from roots in the past. Industrialization irrevocably altered the world, isolating labor from meaningful traditions of handwork and craft. The factory system broke each job into pieces, and man lost sight of the whole. Individualism and competition, high speed and efficient productivity became the new ideals. Anything old, slow, and different was simply outdated or old-fashioned, curious and quaint, perhaps, but irrelevant. The world succeeded in becoming streamlined and modern and, regrettably, older poetic and literary forms were ignored as individuals and nations lost their sense of a meaningful past.

Now as we experience renewed interest in fantasy writing, as contemporary individuals search for collective, unconscious imaginative links with the past, we can turn new eyes to the vision of William Morris. Myths no longer seem distant curiosities and childish fairytales but intriguing imaginative expressions of human transformations and possibilities. *Child Christopher* shares with Morris's other fantasy stories the quality of possessing a vital mythic dimension and provides a unique glimpse of the ancient sources of fantasy. The story unfolds as if we had heard it long ago; yet it is at once fresh and reassuring. It seems to capture and hold fast values, ideas, and feelings which reside at the deep core of human consciousness.

The story of *Child Christopher* actually begins for us, as it did for Morris, with the thirteenth-century English metrical romance, *Havelok the Dane*. *Havelok* was composed in a Northeast Midland dialect of Middle English and is one of the earliest pieces of extant English literature to use the language of the common people and to appeal to a non-courtly audience. Both of these factors would have attracted Morris, who opposed high ranks, pretentious stations, and the social and economic exploitation of the courtly tradition. He recognized in this tale of the exploits of a legendary king of England and Denmark a story with mythic and human importance. Though not widely known, *Havelok* had already served Shakespeare as an inspiration for *Hamlet,* and Morris found his interest whetted by the publication of a new edition of the tale by the Early English Text Society in 1868. Readers may enjoy comparing the Shakespearean and Morrisian treatments, particularly with respect to political, social, and religious attitudes.

The original story tells of an English princess named Goldborough who is left an orphan at the age of two. While she is growing up, her kingdom is to be ruled by a regent appointed by her father. The regent is instructed to marry her to the best, fairest, and strongest man living and to assure her rule as Queen when she is old enough. Instead, he shuts her up in Dover Castle. Parallel to this the hero, Havelok, is orphaned when his father, the King of Denmark, dies. The councilor entrusted to rule until Havelok comes of age attempts to have the young prince drowned, but a luminous mark on the boy's shoulder and a bright light issuing from his mouth convince an honest fisherman that the child must be a true king and he is spirited away to

Chapter I. Of the King of Oakenrealm, & his wife and his child ❀ ❀

O OF old there was a land which was so much a woodland, that a minstrel thereof said it that a squirrel might go from end to end, and all about, from tree to tree, & never touch the earth: therefore was that land called Oakenrealm.

THE lord & king thereof was a stark man, & so great a warrior that in his youth he took no de-

Original first page of text.

Original title page.

England for safekeeping. There Havelok is raised as a simple fisherman. Finally gaining local fame in a sports contest (stone-throwing), he attracts the attention of Goldborough's regent, who decides to marry her to this poor boy. When the two are wed, and both deceitful regents feel their positions to be entirely safe, Havelok and Goldborough realize through dreams and glowing signs that they must claim their thrones. Havelok invades Denmark, regains his kingdom, conquers England, and rewards all those who have cared for him. He and Goldborough live a hundred years and have many children.

In adapting the tale, Morris preferred the happy ending to the discovery of something rotten in Denmark. He advised his daughter the right way of retelling an old romance: "Read it through, then shut the book and write it out again as a new story for yourself." This provides a way of casting the narrative in your own words while preserving the basic spirit of the source. The mixture of early English and old Scandinavian influences in this tale highlighted the cultural roots Morris admired most. He had already followed these roots to the European continent to produce translations of three Old French romances which he published at his Kelmscott Press, starting in 1893. French romance techniques abound in *Child Christopher,* adding yet another important source to the emerging fantasy form. As Joseph Jacobs observed in the introduction to the 1896 edition of Morris's French translations, the historic origins were far-ranging: "Obscure as still remains the origin of that *genre* of romance to which the tales before us belong, there is little doubt that their models, if not their originals, were once extant as Constantinople. Though in no single instance has the Greek original been discovered of any of these romances, the mere name of their heroes would be in most cases sufficient to prove their Hellenic or Byzantine origin." Morris's daughter May suggested a point still more anterior and recognized in these medieval tales elements of folklore traditions as old as human culture, extending to Africa and the East.

The spirit of the original 1895 Kelmscott Press edition is reminiscent of the historical antecedents which inform *Child Christopher.* The title page, with both lettering and floral designs by Morris himself, beautifully combines both Eastern and Western influences and is a fitting place to begin a brief discussion of central themes. (See illustration on facing page.) Morris's vision of unity extended to a wedding of the visual and literary arts: on this title page his achievements as a designer are inextricably bound up with his fantasy vision. Here Morris achieves clear balance in the names of the central characters and directs our attention to levels of meaning within the words. For the sake of his illumination he consciously varies from the official title of the work, *Child Christopher and Goldilind the Fair,* to word his title page "Of Child Christopher and Fair Goldilind." If we read the words in the way Morris has arranged them, we are strongly drawn first to the "Christ" in "Christopher" and the implied spiritual salvation.

As a linguist and translator, Morris was aware of the roots of language as an affirmation of the continuity and progression of human culture. He chose to stress these roots in both his prose style and word choice. The name "Christopher" derives from Greek, through Latin and Old French, and means "bearer of Christ." Originally the word was applied by the Christians to themselves, meaning that they bore Christ in their hearts. Later, St. Christopher came to prominence, an early Christian martyr whose name was attached to the legend of a holy man who carried the child Christ across a river. Always the patron of travellers, St. Christopher was one of the commonest subjects for mural paintings inside English churches and a favorite with the average citizen. Morris, himself not conventionally religious, was attracted by the human emphasis in the story. A Morris and Company stained-glass window depicting Saint Christopher was designed in 1868 by Edward Burne-Jones and executed in rich Morris colors. It is one of the most artistically successful small windows ever executed by the company and emphasizes the human commitment of Christopher, a good man who stooped to carry the burden of a fellow traveller across a difficult impasse. In the context of Morris's tale the name and the image seem clearly to connote human spirituality in relation to one's fellow man.

The central lines of the page provide visual connection and support, with "pher" arranged symmetrically above the following line and hinting at a rhyme between "pher" and "fair." "Gold," normally prompting thoughts of money and material wealth, is joined in the heroine's name with fairness, not greed or exploitation. The spiritual emphasis of Christopher is linked to the material fairness of Goldilind. The final syllables, "ilind," suggest "island" (a reference to England and an old name for Iceland); "I lend," which connotes the supportive dimension Goldilind gives to the union in the book; and "lind," a Middle-English word for tree (used, for instance, by Chaucer in his "Clerk's Tale," "Be ay of chere as light as leef on linde"). This final sense of "tree" leads us to the unifying natural growth motifs present on this title page and throughout the narrative. The language of the page is caressed and embraced but not hidden in natural illumination which ranges from delicate leaf and floral patterns at the center to more vigorous flowing acanthus spirals at the outer border. It shows kinship with the finest Persian illuminated manuscripts and carpets (both of which Morris collected) as well as medieval Celtic and Continental illumination. The page forms a whole, graceful and lively, a wedding of Eastern and Western traditions, of spiritual and material planes, of the unconscious flowing growth of nature with the rational consciousness of language.

We might expect, just from this close examination of the title page, that the narrative will portray an ideal world of natural, human, spiritual balance, and the opening scenes confirm this notion. The book begins in Oakenrealm, a heavily forested country "which was so much a woodland, that a minstrel thereof said it that a squirrel might go from end to end, and all about, from tree to tree, and never touch the earth." In the opening action we find ourselves in a dense wood, but one unlike the dark, confused forest of Dante at the beginning of the *Inferno*. Instead, this wood provides a haven for tiny creatures and focuses our attention on the protective upper branches, like the dome of heaven itself, where our thoughts, with the squirrel, need not touch the earth. While our thoughts are elevated, they are still tied to the earth; supported by the sturdy tree-trunks, unifying branches span the land "from end to end." The imagination is not directed to a distant heaven, but to a higher plane in touch with nature.

This forest kingdom of Oakenrealm is home to Child Christopher, and the trees are symbolic, as they have been from Yggdrasill (in Norse mythology the great ash tree whose roots and branches hold together the universe) to the Christian Tree of Life, suggesting a spiritual as well as a natural domain. Goldilind, despite the "lind" of her name, is from Meadham, an unrising plain close to the earth and therefore suggestive of a material realm. When she encounters Christopher later in the story, it is Goldilind who will be most concerned with appearances and rich position. Though each of these central characters is tagged with the name of a dwelling place, they are both dispossessed of their rightful inheritance and assume functions in opposition to their tag images. In their actions Christopher and Goldilind approximate the archetypal animus and anima of Jungian psychology, the active rational and creative unconscious forces of the psyche. Only when they are united is their success assured, and in their union the spiritual and material, unconscious and conscious, are wed. As political and social commentary, the story suggests the sons and daughters of modern society deprived of their rightful inheritance by corrupt establishments. It illustrates the importance of reuniting the fragmented and dislocated children and affirms the ultimate triumph of their cause.

Morris tells us in his introduction to the Saga Library that in the saga tradition "no detail is spared in impressing the reader with a sense of the reality of the event; but no word is wasted in the process of giving that detail. There is nothing didactic and nothing rhetorical in these stories; the reader is left to make his own commentary on the events, and to divine the motives and feelings of the actors in them without any help from the tale-teller. In short, the simplest and purest form of epical narration." That the reader must "divine" the meaning in the work is a notion both ancient and new. "Divinity" resides neither in an external Godhead nor an omniscient author, but in the intellect and feeling of each reader. Many experimental artists in various media tell us now that their efforts are to involve the spectator fully in the act of creation. In Morris's case, the creative imagination is engaged in action strange and familiar, told in a style which makes events at once real and mythic. Throughout his fantasy writing hidden meanings and significance pop out at us like fairies out of bushes.

That this world should be so like our own and not some totally separate realm of fantasy is an invention which links fantastic events with ordinary realities. It reminds us that we inhabit a significant, myth-making, symbolic reality where coincidence, highly-charged emotion, and idealism mysteriously coalesce; where dreams reveal and foretell factual reality; where truth, once hidden, is finally made plain. Even the parts and components of names have significant roots in human history and myth. We may not realize this as we live day to day, because our minds are so caught up in our humdrum affairs and ordinary language that we do not allow ourselves to consider the other dimension, but here in this fictive realm we find ourselves thinking in symbolism, a mode of comprehension generally lost to civilized man. We experience it only rarely, perhaps in the odd dream we may pause to consider, or in a Freudian slip we are suddenly conscious of having made, or on the analyst's couch, where he may painfully reveal the presence of this other mode to our conscious mind. In Morris's tale characters and readers alike attach deep meanings to both image and action; though they are not explicitly explained, they are implicitly compelling and pressingly felt.

A brief introduction is no place to attempt a full analysis of the symbolic implications of this rich work. Besides, I fully subscribe with Morris to the importance of the notion that "the reader is left to make his own commentary." As in all the best literature, Morris has accomplished here a fusion of politics, morality, art, and invidiual life which challenges our imaginations and elevates our aspirations. It is a happy choice that Newcastle has finally made this book available to a wide reading public, not only because we can now enjoy a happy tale of love and politics set right, but also because it will help us to see more clearly the fusion of influences which stand behind the tradition of the English fantasy novel and which may in turn provide new directions and influences for contemporary fiction.

Richard B. Mathews
Gulfport, Florida, 1976

CHILD CHRISTOPHER AND GOLDILIND THE FAIR

CHAPTER I. OF THE KING OF OAKENREALM, AND HIS WIFE AND HIS CHILD

F old there was a land which was so much a wood-land, that a minstrel thereof said it that a squirrel might go from end to end, and all about, from tree to tree, and never touch the earth: therefore was that land called Oakenrealm.

The lord and king thereof was a stark man, and so great a warrior that in his youth he took no delight in aught else save battle and tourneys. But when he was hard on forty years old, he came across a daughter of a certain lord, whom he had vanquished, and his eyes bewrayed him into longing, so that he gave back to the said lord all the havings he had conquered of him that he might lay the maiden in his kingly bed. So he brought her home with him to Oakenrealm and wedded her.

Tells the tale that he rued not his bargain, but loved her so dearly that for a year round he wore no armour, save when she bade him play in the tilt-yard for her desport and pride. So wore the days till she went with child and was near her time, and then it betid that three kings who marched on Oakenrealm banded them together against him, and his lords and thanes cried out on him to lead them to battle, and it behoved him to do as they would.

So he sent out the tokens and bade an hosting at his chief city, and when all was ready he said farewell to his wife and her babe unborn, and went his ways to battle once more: but fierce was his heart against the foemen, that they had dragged him away from his love and his joy.

Even amidst of his land he joined battle with the host of the ravagers, and the tale of them is short to tell, for they were as the wheat before the hook. But as he followed up the chase, a mere thrall of the fleers turned on him and cast his spear, and it reached him whereas his hawberk was broken, and stood deep in, so that he fell to earth unmighty: and when his lords and chieftains drew about him, and cunning men strove to heal him, it was of no avail, and he knew that his soul was departing. Then he sent for a priest, and for the Marshal of the host, who was a great lord, and the son of his father's brother, and in few words bade him look to the babe whom his wife bore about, and if it were a man, to cherish him and do him to learn all that a king ought to know; and if it were a maiden, that he should look to her wedding well and worthily: and he let swear him on his sword, on the edges and the hilts, that he would do even so, and be true unto his child if child there were: and he bade him have rule, if so be the lords would, and all the people, till the child were of age to be king: and the Marshal swore, and all the lords who stood around bear witness to his swearing. Thereafter the priest houselled the King, and he received his Creator, and a little while after his soul departed.

He gives charge to Rolf the Marshal

He dies

But the Marshal followed up the fleeing foe, and two battles more he fought before he beat them flat to earth; and then they craved for peace, and he went back to the city in mickle honour.

But in the King's city of Oakenham he found but little joy; for both the King was bemoaned, whereas he had been no hard man to his folk; and also, when the tidings and the King's corpse came back to Oakenrealm, his Lady and Queen took sick for sorrow and fear, and fell into labour of her child, and in

The Queen bears a man-child

childing of a man-bairn she died, but the lad lived, and was like to do well.

So there was one funeral for the slain King and for her whom his slaying had slain: and when that was done, the little king was borne to the font, and at his christening he gat to name Christopher.

Homage done to the little King

Thereafter the Marshal summoned all them that were due thereto to come and give homage to the new king, and even so did they, though he were but a babe, yea, and who had but just now been a king lying in his mother's womb. But when the homage was done, then the Marshal called together the wise men, and told them how the King that was had given him in charge his son as then unborn, and the ruling of the realm till the said son were come to man's estate: but he bade them seek one worthier if they had heart to gainsay the word of their dying lord. Then all they said that he was worthy and mighty and the choice of their dear lord, and that they would have none but he.

Rolf lord of the land

So then was the great folk-mote called, and the same matter was laid before all the people, and none said aught against it, whereas no man was ready to name another to that charge and rule, even had it been his own self.

Now then by law was the Marshal, who hight Rolf, lord and earl of the land of Oakenrealm. He ruled well and strongly, and was a fell warrior: he was well befriended by many of the great; and the rest of them feared him and his friends: as for the commonalty, they saw that he held the realm in peace; and for the rest, they knew little and saw less of him, and they paid to his bailiffs and sheriffs as little as they could, and more than they would. But whereas that left them somewhat to grind their teeth on, and they were not harried, they were not so ill content. So the Marshal throve, and lacked nothing of a king's place save the bare name.

He rules mightily

CHAPTER II.   OF THE KING'S SON

A S for the King's son, to whom the folk
had of late done homage as king, he
was at first seen about a corner of the
High House with his nurses; and
then in a while it was said, and the tale noted,
but not much, that he must needs go for his
health's sake, and because he was puny, to
some stead amongst the fields, and folk heard
say that he was gone to the strong house of
a knight somewhat stricken in years, who was
called Lord . Richard the Lean.   The said
house was some twelve miles from Oakenham,
not far from the northern edge of the wild-wood.
But in a while, scarce more than a year, Lord
Richard brake up house at the said castle, and
went southward through the forest.   Of this
departure was little said, for he was not a man
amongst the foremost.   As for the King's little
son, if any remembered that he was in the
hands of the said Lord Richard, none said
aught about it; for if any thought of the little
babe at all, they said to themselves, Never
will he come to be king.

Now as for Lord Richard the Lean, he went
far through the wood, and until he was come
to another house of his, that stood in a clearing

somewhat near to where Oakenrealm marched on another country, which hight Meadham; though the said wild-wood ended not where Oakenrealm ended, but stretched a good way into Meadham; and betwixt one and the other much rough country there was.

He goes far away from the King's seat

It is to be said that amongst those who went to this stronghold of the woods was the little King Christopher, no longer puny, but a stout babe enough: so he was borne amongst the serving-men and thralls to the Castle of the Outer March; and he was in nowise treated as a great man's son; but there was more than one woman who was kind to him, and as he waxed in strength and beauty month by month, both carle and quean fell to noting him, and, for as little as he was, he began to be well-beloved.

Christopher a fair babe

As to the stead where he was nourished, though it were far away amongst the woods, it was no such lonely or savage place: besides the castle and the houses of it, there was a merry thorpe in the clearing the houses thereof were set down by the side of a clear and pleasant little stream. Moreover, the goodmen and swains of the said township were no ill folk, but bold of heart, free of speech, and goodly of favour; and the women of them fair, kind, and trusty. Whiles came folk journeying in to Oakenrealm or out to Meadham, and of

Of the stead where he dwelt

these some were minstrels, who had with them tidings of what was astir whereas folk were thicker in the world, and some chapmen, who chaffered with the thorpe-dwellers, and took of them the wood-land spoil for such outland goods as those woodmen needed.

Christopher forgotten at court

So wore the years, and in Oakenham King Christopher was well nigh forgotten, and in the wild-wood had never been known clearly for King's son. At first, by command of Rolf the Marshal, a messenger came every year from Lord Richard with a letter that told of how the lad Christopher did. But when five years were worn, the Marshal bade send him tidings thereof every three years; and by then it was come to the twelfth year, and still the tidings were that the lad throve ever, and meanwhile the Marshal sat fast in his seat

The messengers cease

with none to gainsay, the word went to Lord Richard that he should send no more, for that he, the Marshal, had heard enough of the boy; that if he throve it were well, and if not, it was no worse. So wore the days and the years.

CHAPTER III. OF THE KING OF MEADHAM AND HIS DAUGHTER

TELLS the tale that in the country which lay south of Oakenrealm, and was called Meadham, there was in these days a king whose wife was dead, but had left him a fair daughter, who was born some four years after King Christopher. A good man was this King Roland, mild, bounteous, and no regarder of persons in his justice; and well-beloved he was of his folk: yet could not their love keep him alive; for, whenas his daughter was of the age of twelve years, he sickened unto death; and so, when he knew that his end drew near, he sent for the wisest of his wise men, and they came unto him sorrowing in the High House of his chiefest city, which hight Meadhamstead. So he bade them sit down nigh unto his bed, and took up the word and spake:

Masters, and my good lords, ye may see clearly that a sundering is at hand, and that I must needs make a long journey, whence I shall come back never; now I would, and am verily of duty bound thereto, that I leave behind me some good order in the land. Furthermore, I would that my daughter, when she

King Roland a good man

He falls sick

He tells of his daughter

is of age thereto, should be Queen in Meadham, and rule the land; neither will it be many years before she shall be of ripe age for ruling, if ever she may be; and I deem not that there shall be any lack in her, whereas her mother could all courtesy, and was as wise as a woman may be. But how say ye, my masters?

So they all with one consent said Yea, and they would ask for no better king than their lady his daughter. Then said the King:

He takes rede of his wisemen

Hearken carefully, for my time is short: Yet is she young and a maiden, though she be wise. Now therefore do I need some man well looked to of the folk, who shall rule the land in her name till she be of eighteen winters, and who shall be her good friend and counsellor into all wisdom thereafter. Which of you, my masters, is meet for this matter?

They speak

Then they all looked one on the other, and spake not. And the King said: Speak, some one of you, without fear; this is no time for tarrying. Thereon spake an elder, the oldest of them, and said: Lord, this is the very truth, that none of us here present are meet for this office: whereas, among other matters, we be all unmeet for battle; some of us have never been warriors, and other some are past the age for leading an host. To say the sooth, King, there is but one man in Meadham who may do what thou wilt, and not fail; both for

They tell Earl Geoffrey as the one man for Vice-King

his wisdom, and his might afield, and the account which is had of him amongst the people; and that man is Earl Geoffrey, of the Southern Marches.

Ye say sooth, quoth the King; but is he down in the South or nigher to hand? Said the elder: He is as now in Meadhamstead, and may be in this chamber in scant half an hour. So the King bade send for him, and there was silence in the chamber till he came in, clad in a scarlet kirtle and a white cloak, and with his sword by his side. He was a tall man, bigly made; somewhat pale of face, black and curly of hair; blue-eyed, and thin-lipped, and hook-nosed as an eagle; a man warrior-like, and somewhat fierce of aspect. He knelt down by the King's bedside, and asked him in a sorrowful voice what he would, and the King said: I ask a great matter of thee, and all these my wise men, and I myself, withal, deem that thou canst do it, and thou alone ... nay, hearken: I am departing, and I would have thee hold my place, and do unto my people even what I would do if I myself were living; and to my daughter as nigh to that as may be. I say all this thou mayest do, if thou wilt be as trusty and leal to me after I am dead, as thou hast seemed to all men's eyes to have been while I was living. What sayest thou?

The King gives him charge

The Earl had hidden his face in the coverlet of the bed while the King was speaking; but now he lifted up his face, weeping, and said: Kinsman and friend and King; this is nought hard to do; but if it were, yet would I do it. It is well, said the King: my heart fails me and my voice; so give heed, and set thine ear close to my mouth: hearken, belike my daughter Goldilind shall be one of the fairest of women; I bid thee wed her to the fairest of men and the strongest, and to none other.

Thereat his voice failed him indeed, and he lay still; but he died not, till presently the priest came to him, and, as he might, houselled him: then he departed.

As for Earl Geoffrey, when the King was buried, and the homages done to the maiden Goldilind, he did no worse than those wise men deemed of him, but bestirred him, and looked full sagely into all the matters of the kingdom, and did so well therein that all men praised his rule perforce, whether they loved him or not; and sooth to say he was not much beloved.

CHAPTER IV. OF THE MAIDEN GOLDILIND

AMIDST of all his other business Earl Geoffrey bethought him in a while of the dead King's daughter, and he gave her in charge to a gentlewoman, somewhat stricken in years, a widow of high lineage, but not over wealthy. She dwelt in her own house in a fair valley some twenty miles from Meadhamstead: there abode Goldilind till a year and a half was worn, and had due observance, but little love, and not much kindness from the said gentlewoman, who hight Dame Elinor Leashowe. Howbeit, time and again came knights and ladies and lords to see the little lady, and kissed her hand and did obeisance to her; yet more came to her in the first three months of her sojourn at Leashowe than the second, and more in the second than the third.

At last, on a day when the said year and a half was fully worn, thither came Earl Geoffrey with a company of knights and men-at-arms, and he did obeisance, as due was, to his master's daughter, and then spake awhile privily with Dame Elinor; and thereafter they went into the hall, he, and she, and Goldilind,

Of Goldilind

Of Goldilind's governante

Earl Geoffrey comes to Leashowe

and there before all men he spake aloud and said. My Lady Goldilind, meseemeth ye dwell here all too straightly; for neither is this house of Leashowe great enough for thy state, and the entertainment of the knights and lords who shall have will to seek to thee hither; nor is the wealth of thy liege dame and governante as great as it should be, and as thou, meseemeth, wouldst have it. Wherefore I have been considering thy desires herein, and if thou deem it meet to give a gift to Dame Elinor, and live queenlier thyself than now thou dost, then mayst thou give unto her the Castle of *He tells of* Greenharbour, and the six manors appertain-*Green-* ing thereto, and withal the rights of wild-wood *harbour* and fen and fell that lie thereabout. Also, if thou wilt, thou mayst honour the said castle with abiding there awhile at thy pleasure; and I shall see to it that thou have due meney to go with thee thither. How sayest thou my lady?

Amongst that company there were two or three who looked at each other and half smiled; and two or three looked on the maiden, who was goodly as of her years, as if with compassion; but the more part kept countenance in full courtly wise.

Goldilind Then spake Goldilind in a quavering voice *answers* (for she was afraid and wise), and she said: Cousin and Earl, we will that all this be done; and it likes me well to eke the wealth of this lady and my good friend Dame Elinor. Quoth Earl Geoffrey: Kneel before thy lady, dame, and put thine hands between hers and thank her for the gift. So Dame Elinor knelt down, and did homage and obeisance for her new land; and Goldilind raised her up and kissed her, and bade her sit down beside her, and spake to her kindly; and all men praised the maiden for her gentle and courteous ways; and Dame Elinor smiled upon her and them, what she could. She was small of body and sleek; but her cheeks somewhat flagging; brown eyes she had, long, half opened; thin lips, and chin somewhat falling away from her mouth; hard on fifty winters had she seen; yet there have been those who were older and goodlier both.

A gift for Dame Elinor

Of Dame Elinor's aspect

CHAPTER V. GOLDILIND COMES TO GREENHARBOUR

BUT a little while tarried the Earl Geoffrey at Leashowe, but departed next morning and came to Meadhamstead. A month thereafter came folk from him to Leashowe, to wit, the new meney for the new abode of Goldilind; amongst whom was a goodly band of men-at-arms, led by an old lord pinched and peevish of face, who kneeled to Goldilind as the new burgreve of Greenharbour; and a chaplain, a black canon, young, broad-cheeked and fresh-looking, but hard-faced and unlovely; three new damsels withal were come for the young Queen, not young maids, but stalworth women, well grown, and two of them hard-featured; the third, tall, black-haired, and a goodly-fashioned body.

Now when these were come, who were all under the rule of Dame Elinor, there was no gainsaying the departure to the new home; and in two days' time they went their ways from Leashowe. But though Goldilind was young, she was wise, and her heart misgave her, when she was amidst this new meney, that she was not riding toward glory and honour, and a world of worship and friends beloved.

Howbeit, whatso might lie before her, she put a good face upon it, and did to those about her queenly and with all courtesy.

Five days they rode from Leashowe north away, by thorpe and town and mead and river, till the land became little peopled, and the sixth day they rode the wild-wood ways, where was no folk, save now and again the little cot of some forester or collier; but the seventh day, about noon, they came into a clearing of the wood, a rugged little plain of lea-land, mingled with marish, with a little deal of acre-land in barley and rye, round about a score of poor frame-houses set down scatter-meal about the lea. But on a long ridge, at the northern end of the said plain, was a grey castle, strong, and with big and high towers, yet not so much greater than was Leashowe, deemed Goldilind, as for a dwelling-house.

A poor land

Howbeit, they entered the said castle, and within, as without, it was somewhat grim, though nought was lacking of plenishing due for folk knightly. Long it were to tell of its walls and baileys and chambers; but let this suffice, that on the north side, toward the thick forest, was a garden of greensward and flowers and potherbs; and a garth-wall of grey stone, not very high, was the only defence thereof toward the wood, but it was overlooked by a tall tower of the great wall, which hight the

The Castle of Green-harbour

Foresters' Tower. In the said outer garth-wall also was a postern, whereby there was not seldom coming in and going out.

*Goldilind
a prisoner*

Now when Goldilind had been in her chamber for a few days, she found out for certain, what she had before misdoubted, that she had been brought from Leashowe and the peopled parts near to Meadhamstead unto the uttermost parts of the realm to be kept in prison there.

*She is kept
somewhat
close*

Howbeit, it was in a way prison courteous; she was still served with observance, and bowed before, and called my lady and queen, and so forth: also she might go from chamber to hall and chapel, to and fro, yet scarce alone; and into the garden she might go, yet not for the more part unaccompanied; and even at whiles she went out a-gates, but then ever with folk on the right hand and the left. Forsooth, whiles and again, within the next two years of her abode at Greenharbour, out of gates she went and alone; but that was as the prisoner who strives to be free (although she had, forsooth, no thought or hope of escape), and as the prisoner brought back was she chastised when she came within gates again. Everywhere, to be short, within and about the Castle of Greenharbour, did Goldilind meet the will and the tyranny of the little sleek widow, Dame Elinor, to whom both carle and quean in that corner of the world were but as servants and slaves to do her will; and the said Elinor, who at first was but spiteful in word and look toward her lady, waxed worse as time *Dame* wore and as the blossom of the King's daugh- *Elinor's* ter's womanhood began to unfold, till at last the *tyranny* she-jailer had scarce feasted any day when she had not in some wise grieved and tormented her prisoner; and whatever she did, none had might to say her nay.

But Goldilind took all with a high heart, *She makes* and her courage grew with her years, nor *the best* would she bow the head before any grief, but *of it* took to her whatsoever solace might come to her; as the pleasure of the sun and the wind, and the beholding of the greenery of the wood, and the fowl and beasts playing, which oft she saw afar, and whiles anear, though whiles, forsooth, she saw nought of it all, whereas she was shut up betwixt four walls, and that not of her chamber, but of some bare and foul prison of the Castle, which, with other griefs, must she needs thole under the name and guise of penance.

However, she waxed so exceeding fair and *Goldilind* sweet and lovely, that the loveliness of her *waxeth* pierced to the hearts of many of her jailers, so *very fair* that some of them, and specially of the squires and men-at-arms, would do her some easement which they might do unrebuked, or not sorely rebuked; as bringing her flowers in the spring, or whiles a singing-bird or a squirrel; and an

old man there was of the men-at-arms, who would ask leave, and get it at whiles, to come to her in her chamber, or the garden, and tell her minstrel tales and the like for her joyance. Sooth to say, even the pinched heart of the old Burgreve was somewhat touched by her; and he alone had any might to stand between her and Dame Elinor; so that but for him it had gone much harder with her than it did.

For the rest, none entered the Castle from the world without, nay not so much as a travelling monk, or a friar on his wanderings, save and except some messenger of Earl Geoffrey who had errand with Dame Elinor or the Burgreve.

So wore the days and the seasons, till it was now more than four years since she had left Leashowe, and her eighteenth summer was beginning. But now the tale leaves telling of Goldilind, and goes back to the matters of Oakenrealm, and therein to what has to do with King Christopher and Rolf the Marshal.

CHAPTER VI. HOW ROLF THE MARSHAL DREAMS A DREAM AND COMES TO THE CASTLE OF THE UTTERMOST MARCH

NOW this same summer, when King Christopher was of twenty years and two, Rolf the Marshal, sleeping one noontide in the King's garden at Oakenham, dreamed a dream. For himseemed that there came through the garth-gate a woman fair and tall, and clad in nought but oaken-leaves, who led by the hand an exceeding goodly young man of twenty summers, and his visage like to the last battle-dead King of Oakenrealm when he was a young man. And the said woman led the swain up to the Marshal, who asked in his mind what these two were: and the woman answered his thought and said. I am the Woman of the Woods, and the Land-wight of Oakenrealm; and this lovely lad whose hand I hold is my King and thy King and the King of Oakenrealm. Wake, fool . . . wake! and look to it what thou wilt do! And therewith he woke up crying out, and drew forth his sword. But when he was fully awakened, he was ashamed, and went into the hall, and sat in his high-seat, and strove to

Of a dream

The Land-wight of Oakenrealm

*The
dream
dreamed
again*

think out of his troubled mind; but for all he might do, he fell asleep again; and again in the hall he dreamed as he had dreamed in the garden: and when he awoke from his dream he had no thought in his head but how he might the speediest come to the house of Lord Richard the Lean, and look to the matter of his lord's son and see him with his eyes, and, if it might be, take some measure with the threat which lay in the lad's life. Nought he tarried, but set off in an hour's time with no more company than four men-at-arms and an old squire of his, who was wont to do his bidding without question, whether it were good or evil. So they went by frith and fell, by wood and fair ways, till in two days' time they were come by undern within sight of the Castle of the Outer March, and entered into the street of the thorpe aforesaid; and they saw that there were no folk therein, and at the house-doors save old carles and carlines scarce wayworthy, and little children who might not go afoot. But from the field anigh the thorpe came the sound of shouting and glad voices, and through the lanes of the houses they saw on the field many people in gay raiment going to and fro, as though there were games and sports toward.

*Lord
Rolf will
see the
youngling*

*The
thorpe
of the
Outer
March*

Thereof Lord Rolf heeded nought, but went his ways straight to the Castle, and was brought with all honour into the hall, and thither came Lord Robert the Lean, hastening and half afeard, and did obeisance to him; and there were but a few in the hall, and they stood out of earshot of the two lords. The Marshal spoke graciously to Lord Richard, and made him sit beside him, and said in a soft voice: We have come to see thee, Lord, and how the folk do in the Uttermost Marches. Also we would wot how it goes with a lad whom we sent to thee when he was yet a babe, whereas he was some byblow of the late King, our lord and master, and we deemed thee both rich enough and kind enough to breed him into thriving without increasing pride upon him: and, firstly, is the lad yet alive?

He knitted his brow as he spake, for carefulness of soul; but Lord Richard smiled upon him, though as one somewhat troubled, and answered: Lord Marshal, I thank thee for visiting this poor house; and I shall tell thee first that the lad lives, and hath thriven marvellously, though he be somewhat unruly, and will abide no correction now these last six years. Sooth to say, there is now no story of his being anywise akin to our late Lord King; though true it is that the folk in this far-away corner of the land call him King Christopher, but only in a manner of jesting. But it is no jest wherein they say that they will gainsay him nought, and that especially the young

Lord Rolf and Lord Richard

Lord Richard tells of the youngling

Of Christopher and his prowess

women. Yet I will say of him that he is wise, and asketh not overmuch; the more is the sorrow of many of the maidens. A fell woodsman he is, and exceeding stark, and as yet heedeth more of valiance than of the love of woman.

Christopher sent for

The Marshal looked no less troubled than before at these words; he said: I would see this young man speedily. So shall it be, Lord, said Lord Richard. Therewith he called to him a squire, and said: Go thou down into the thorpe, and bring hither Christopher, for that a great lord is here who would set him to do a deed of woodcraft, such as is more than the wont of men.

He cometh with a company

So the squire went his ways, and was gone a little while, and meantime drew nigh to the hall and sound of triumphing songs and shouts, and right up to the hall doors; then entered the squire, and by his side came a tall young man, clad but in a white linen shirt and deerskin brogues, his head crowned with a garland of flowers: him the squire brought up to the lords on the dais, and louted to them, and said: My lords, I bring you Christopher, and he not over willing, for now hath he been but just crowned king of the games down yonder; but when the carles and queans there said that they would come with him and bear him company to the hall doors, then, forsooth, he yea-said the coming. It were not unmeet that some shame were done him.

Peace man! said Lord Richard, what hath this to do with thee? Seest thou not the Lord Marshal here? The Lord Rolf sat and gazed on the lad, and scowled on him; but Christopher saw therein nought but the face of a great lord burdened with many cares; so when he had made his obeisance he stood up fearlessly and merrily before them.

Christopher before the Earl Marshal

Sooth to say, he was full fair to look on: for all his strength, which, as ye shall hear, was mighty, all the fashion of his limbs and his body was light and clean done, and beauteous; and though his skin, where it showed naked, was all tanned with the summer, it was fine and sleek and kindly, every deal thereof: bright-eyed and round-cheeked he was, with full lips and carven chin, and his hair golden brown of hue, and curling crisp about the blossoms of his garland.

The like of him told of

So must we say that he was such an youngling as most might have been in the world, had not man's malice been, and the mischief of grudging and the marring of grasping.

But now spake Lord Rolf: Sir varlet, they tell me that thou art a mighty hunter, and of mickle guile in woodcraft; wilt thou then hunt somewhat for me, and bring me home a catch seldom seen? Yea, Lord King, said Christo-

The Marshal would send him an errand

pher, I will at least do my best, if thou but tell me where to seek the quarry and when. It is well, said the Marshal, and to-morrow my squire, whom thou seest yonder, and who hight Simon, shall tell thee where the hunt is up, and thou shalt go with him. But hearken! thou shalt not call me king; for to-day there is no king in Oakenrealm, and I am but Marshal, and Earl of the king that shall be.

Christopher hath a memory

The lad fell a-musing for a minute, and then he said: Yea, Lord Marshal, I shall do thy will: but meseemeth I have heard some tale of one who was but of late king in Oakenrealm: is it not so, Lord? Stint thy talk, young man, cried the Marshal in a harsh voice, and abide to-morrow; who knoweth who shall be king, and whether thou or I shall live to see him.

The Marshal gives him a ring

But as he spake the words they seemed to his heart like a foretelling of evil, and he turned pale and trembled, and said to Christopher: Come hither, lad; I will give thee a gift, and then shalt thou depart till to-morrow. So Christopher drew near to him, and the Marshal pulled off a ring from his finger and set it on the lad's, and said to him: Now depart in peace; and Christopher bent the knee to him and thanked him for the gracious gift of the ruler of Oakenrealm, and then went his ways out of the hall, and the folk without gave a glad cry as he came amongst them.

But by then he was come to the door, Lord Rolf looked on his hand, and saw that, instead of giving the youngling a finger-ring which he had bought of a merchant for a price of five bezants, as he had meant to do, he had given him a ring which the old King had had, whereon was the first letter of his name (Christopher to wit), and a device of a crowned rose, for this ring was a signet of his. Wherefore was the Marshal once more sore troubled, and he arose, and was half minded to run down the hall after Christopher; but he refrained him, and presently smiled to himself, and then fell a-talking to Lord Richard, sweetly and pleasantly.

The like of the ring

So wore the day to evening; but, ere he went to bed, the Lord Rolf had a privy talk, first with Lord Richard, and after with his squire Simon. What followed of that talk ye may hear after.

Of privy talk

CHAPTER VII. HOW CHRISTOPHER WENT A JOURNEY INTO THE WILD-WOOD

*Chris-
topher
boun
for the
way*

NEXT morning Christopher, who slept in the little hall of the inner court of the Castle, arose betimes, and came to the great gate; but, for as early as he was, there he saw the squire Simon abiding him, standing between two strong horses; to him he gave the sele of the day, and the squire greeted him, but in somewhat surly wise. Then he said to him: Well, King Christopher, art thou ready for the road? Yea, as thou seest, said the youngling smiling. For, indeed,

His attire

he had breeches now beneath his shirt, and a surcoat of green woollen over it; boots of deer-skin had he withal, and spurs thereon: he was girt with a short sword, and had a quiver of arrows at his back, and bare a great bow in his hand.

*Chris-
topher
and
Squire
Simon*

Yea, quoth Simon, thou deemest thee a gay swain belike; but thou lookest likelier for a deerstealer than a rider; thou, hung up to thy shooting-gear. Deemest thou we go a-hunting of the hind? Quoth Christopher: I wot not, squire; but the great lord, who lieth sleeping yonder, hath told me that thou shouldest give me his errand; and of some hunting or feat of woodcraft he spake. Moreover, this crooked stick can drive a shaft through matters harder than a hind's side. Simon looked confused, and he reddened and stammered somewhat as he answered: Ah, yea: so it was; I mind me; I *An answer* will tell thee anon. Said Christopher: Withal, squire, if we are wending into the wood, as needs we must, unless we ride round about this dale in a ring all day, dost thou deem we shall go a gallop many a mile? Nay, fair sir; the horses shall wend a foot's pace oftenest, and we shall go a-foot not unseldom through the thickets. Now was Simon come to himself again, and that self was surly, so he said: Ay, ay, little King, thou deemest thee exceeding wise in these woods, dost thou not? and, forsooth, thou mayst be. Yet have I tidings for thee. Yea, and what be they? said Christopher. Simon grinned: Even these, said he, *A jest* that Dr. Knowall was no man's cousin while he lived, and that he died last week. Therewith he swung himself into his saddle, and Christopher laughed merrily at his poor gibe and mounted in like wise.

Therewithal they rode their ways through *Of the* the thorpe, and at the southern end thereof *road* Simon drew rein, and looked on Christopher as if he would ask him something, but asked not. Then said Christopher: Whither go we now?

Said Simon: It is partly for thee to say:
hearken, I am bidden first to ride the Redwater
Wood with thee: knowest thou that? Yea,
said the lad, full well: but which way shall we
ride it? Wilt thou come out of it at Redwater
Head, or Herne Moss, or the Long Pools?
Said Simon: We shall make for the Long
Pools, if thou canst bring me there. Christopher laughed: Aha! said he, then am I some
far-away cousin of Dr. Knowall when the
whole tale is told: forsooth I can lead thee
thither; but tell me, what shall I do of valiant
deeds at the Long Pools? for there is no fire-
drake nor effit, nay, nor no giant, nor guileful
dwarf, nought save mallard and coot, heron and
bittern; yea, and ague-shivers to boot. Simon
looked sourly on him and said: Thou art bidden
to go with me, young man, or gainsay the Marshal. Art thou mighty enough thereto? For
the rest, fear not but that the deed shall come
to thee one day. Nay, said Christopher, it is
all one to me, for I am at home in these woods
and wastes, I and my shafts. Tell me of the
deeds when thou wilt. But inwardly he longed
to know the deed, and fretted him because
of Simon's surliness and closeness. Then he
said: Well, Squire Simon, let us to the road;
for thou shalt know that to-night we must
needs house us under the naked heaven; in
nowise can we come to the Long Pools before

to-morrow morning. Yea, and why not? said the squire; I have lain in worse places. Wilt thou tell me thereof? said Christopher. Mayhappen, said Simon, if to-morrow comes and goes for both of us twain.

So they rode their ways through the wood, *Of* and baited at midday with what Simon bare in *lodging* his saddle-bags, and then went on till night fell on them; then asked Simon how long they were from the Long Pools, and Christopher told him that they were yet short of them some fifteen miles, and those long ones, because of the marish grounds. So they tethered their horses there and ate their supper; and lay down to sleep in the house of the woods, by a fire-side which they lighted.

But in the midnight Christopher, who was *An* exceeding fine-eared, had an inkling of some- *awaken-* one moving afoot anigh him, and he awoke *ing* therewith, and sprang up, his drawn short-sword in his hand, and found himself face to face with Simon, and he also with his sword drawn. Simon sprang aback, but held up his sword-point, and Christopher, not yet fully awake, cried out: What wouldst thou? What is it? Simon answered, stammering and all *Of a* abashed: Didst thou not hear then? it wakened *noise* me. I heard nought, said Christopher; what was it? Horses going in the wood, said Simon. Ah, yea, said Christopher, it will have been the

wild colts and the mares; they harbour about
these marsh-land parts. Go to sleep again,
neighbour, the night is not yet half worn; but
I will watch a while. Then Simon sheathed
his sword, and turned about and stood uneasily
a little while, and then cast him down as one
who would sleep hastily; but slept not forsooth,
though he presently made semblance of it: as
for Christopher, he drew together the brands
of the fire, and sat beside it with his blade
over his knees, until the first beginning of the
summer dawn was in the sky; then he began to
nod, and presently lay aback and slept soundly.
Simon slept not, but durst not move. So they
lay till it was broad day, and the sunbeams
came thrusting through the boughs of the
thicket.

CHAPTER VIII. CHRISTOPHER COMES TO THE TOFTS

WHEN they arose in the sunshine, Simon went straight-way to see to the horses, while Christopher stayed by the fire to dight their victuals; he was merry enough, and sang to himself the while; but when Simon came back again, Christopher looked on him sharply, but for a while Simon would not meet his eye, though he asked divers questions of him concerning little matters, as though he were fain to hear Christopher's voice; at last he raised his eyes, and looked on him steadily, and then Christopher said: Well, wayfarer mine, and whither away this morning? Said Simon: As thou wottest, to the Long Pools. Said the lad: Well, thou keepest thy tidings so close, that I will ask thee no more till we come to the Long Pools; since there, forsooth, thou must needs tell me; unless we sunder company there, whereof I were nought grieving. Mayhappen thou shalt fare a long way to-day, muttered Simon. But the lad cried out aloud, while his eye glittered and his cheek flushed: Belike thou hadst well-nigh opened the door thereto last night! And therewith he leapt to

Morning in the wood

Of the road again

his feet and drew his short-sword, and with three deft strokes sheared asunder an over-hanging beech-bough as thick as a man's wrist, that it fell crashing down, and caught Simon amongst the fall of its leafy twigs, while Christopher stood laughing on him, but with a dangerous lofty look in his eyes: then he turned away quietly toward the horses and mounted his nag, and Simon followed and did the like, silently; crestfallen he looked, with brooding fierceness in his face.

So they rode their ways, and spake but little each to each till they came to where the trees of the wood thinned speedily, and gave out at last at the foot of a low stony slope but little grassed; and when they had ridden up to the brow and could see below, Christopher stretched out his hand, and said: Lo thou the Long Pools, fellow wayfarer! and lo some of the tramping horses that woke thee and not me last night. Forsooth there lay below them a great stretch of grass, which whiles ran into mere quagmire, and whiles was sound and better grassed; and the said plain was seamed

by three long shallow pools, with, as it were, grassy causeways between them, grown over here and there with ancient alder trees; but the stony slope whereon they had reined up bent round the plain mostly to the east, as though it were the shore of a great water; and

far away to the south the hills of the forest
rose up blue, and not so low at the most, but
that they were somewhat higher than the crest
of the White Horse as ye may see it from the
little Berkshire hills above the Thames. Down
on the firm greensward there was indeed a herd
of wild horses feeding; mallard and coot swam
about the waters; the whimbrel laughed from
the bent-sides, and three herons stood on the
side of the causeway seeking a good fishing-
stead.

Simon sat a-horseback looking askance from
the marish to Christopher, and said nothing a
while; then he spake in a low croaking voice,
and said: So, little King, we have come to the
Long Pools; now I will ask thee, hast thou
been further southward than this marish land?
That have I, said the lad, a day's journey
further; but according to the tales of men it
was at the peril of my life. Simon seemed as
if he had not noted his last word; he said:
Well then, since thou knowest the wild and
the wood, knowest thou amidst of the thickets
there, two lumps of bare hills, like bowls turned
bottom up, that rise above the trees, and on
each a tower, and betwixt them a long house.

Save us, Allhallows! quoth Christopher, but
thou wilt mean the Tofts! Is it so, sir squire?
Even so, said Simon. And thou knowest what
dwelleth there, and wouldst have me lead thee

*They
stay
some-
what*

*A
question
and its
answer*

thither? said the lad. I am so bidden, said Simon; if thou wilt not do my bidding, seek thou some place to hide thee in from the hand of the Earl Marshal. Said the youngling: Knowest thou not Jack of the Tofts and his seven sons, and what he is, and that he dwelleth there? Said Simon: I know of him; yea, and himself I know, and that he dwelleth there; and I wot that men call him an outlaw, and that many rich men shall lack ere he lacks. What then? This, said Christopher, that, as all tales tell, he will take my life if I ride thither. And, said he, turning on Simon, this is belike what thou wouldest with me? And therewith he drew out his sword, for his bow was unstrung.

A challenge

But Simon sat still and let his sword abide, and said, sourly enough: Thou art a fool to think I am training thee to thy death by him; for I have no will to die, and why shall he not slay me also? Now again I say unto thee, thou hast the choice, either to lead me to the Tofts, where shall be the deed for thee to do, or to hide thee in some hole, as I said afore, from the vengeance of the Lord of Oaken-realm. But as for thy sword, thou mayst put it up, for I will not fight with thee, but rather let thee go with a string to thy leg, if thou wilt not be wise and do as thy lords ordain for thee.

Simon will not fight

Christopher sheathed his sword, and a smile

came into his face, as if some new thought were stirring in him, and he said: Well, since thou wilt not fight with me, and I but a lad, I will e'en do thy will and thine errand to Jack of the Tofts. Maybe he is not so black as he is painted, and not all tales told of him are true. But some of them I will tell thee as we ride along. And some thereof I know already, O wood-land knight, said Simon, as they rode down the bent, and Christopher led on toward the green causeway betwixt the waters. Tell me, quoth he, when they had ridden awhile, is this one of thy tales, how Jack of the Tofts went to the Yule feast of a great baron in the guise of a minstrel, and, even as they bore in the boar's head, smote the said baron on the neck, so that his head lay by the head of the swine on the Christmas board?

Yea, said Christopher, and how Jack cried out: Two heads of swine, one good to eat, one good to burn. But, my master, thou shalt know that this manslaying was not for nought: whereas the Baron of Greenlake had erewhile slain Jack's father in felon wise, where he could strike no stroke for life; and two of his brethren also had he slain, and made the said Jack an outlaw, and he all sackless. In the Uttermost March we deem that he had a case against the baron.

Hah! said Simon. Is this next tale true,

Yet more tales

that this Jack o' the Tofts slew a good knight before the altar, so that the priest's mass-hackle was all wet with his blood, whereas the said priest was in act of putting the holy body into the open mouth of the said knight?

The cause

Christopher said eagerly: True was it, by the Rood! and well was it done! For that same Sir Raoul was an ugly traitor, who had knelt down where he died to wed the Body of the Lord to a foul lie in his mouth; whereas the man who knelt beside him he had trained to his destruction, and was even then doing the first deal of his treason by forswearing him there.

And that man who knelt with him there, said Simon, what betid to him? Said Christopher: He went out of the church with Jack of the Tofts that minute of the stroke; and to the Tofts he went with him, and abode with him freely: and a valiant man he was . . . and is.

Another tale

Hah! said Simon again. And then there is this: that the seven sons of Jack of the Tofts bore off perforce four fair maidens of gentle blood from the castle wherein they dwelt, serving a high dame in all honour; and that, moreover, they hanged the said dame over the battlements of her own castle. Is this true, fair sir?

True is it as the gospel, said Christopher: yet many say that the hanged dame had somewhat less than her deserts; for a foul and cruel whore had she been; and had done many to be done to death, and stood by while they were pined. And the like had she done with those four damsels, had there not been the stout sons of Jack of the Tofts; so that the dear maidens were somewhat more than willing to be borne away.

Where-fore it was

Simon grinned: Well lad, said he, I see that thou knowest Jack of the Tofts even better than I do; so why in the devil's name thou art loth to lead me to him, I wot not.

Christopher reddened, and held his peace awhile; then he said: Well fellow-farer, at least I shall know something of him ere next midnight. Yea, said Simon, and shall we not come to the Tofts before nightfall? Let us essay it, said Christopher, and do our best, it yet lacketh three hours of noon. Therewith he spurred on, for the greensward was hard under the hooves, and they had yet some way to go before they should come amongst the trees and thickets.

They spur for the Tofts

Into the said wood they came, and rode all day diligently, but night fell on them before they saw either house or man or devil; then said Simon: Why should we go any further before dawn? Will it not be best to come to this perilous house by daylight? Said Christopher: There be perils in the wood as

Night cometh

well as in the house. If we lie down here, maybe Jack's folk may come upon us sleeping, and some mischance may befall us. Withal, hereabout be no wild horses to wake thee and warn thee of thy foeman anigh. Let us press on; there is a moon, though she be somewhat hidden by clouds, and meseemeth the way lieth clear before me; neither are we a great way from the Tofts.

Simon craveth somewhat

Then Simon rode close up to Christopher, and took his rein and stayed him, and said to him, as one who prayeth: Young man, willest thou my death? That is as it may be, said Christopher; willest thou mine? Simon held his peace awhile, and Christopher might not see what was in his face amidst the gathering dusk; but he twitched his rein out of the squire's hand, as if he would hasten onward; then the squire said: Nay, I pray thee abide and hear a word of me. Speak then, said Christopher, but hasten, for I hunger, and I would we were in the hall. And therewith he laughed. Said Simon: Thus it is: If I go back to my lord, and bear no token of having done his errand to Jack of the Tofts, then am I in evil case; and if I come to the Tofts, I wot well that Jack is a man fierce of heart, and ready of hand: now, therefore, I pray thee give me thy word to be my warrant, so far as thou mayst be, with this woodman and his sons.

Simon would have warrant of safety

At that word Christopher brake out a-laughing loudly, till all the dusk wood rang with the merry sound of his fresh voice; at last he said: Well, well, thou art but a craven to be a secret murderer: the Lord God would have had an easy bargain of Cain, had he been such as thou. Come on, and do thine errand to Jack of the Tofts, and I will hold thee harmless, so far as I may. Though, sooth to say, I guessed what thine errand was, after the horses waked thee and put a naked sword in thine hand last night. Marry! I had no inkling of it when we left the Castle yesterday morning, but deemed thy lord needed me to do him some service. Come on then! or rather go thou on before me a pace; there, where thou seest the glimmer betwixt the beech-trees yonder; if thou goest astray, I am anigh thee for a guide. And I say that we shall not go far without tidings.

Simon went on perforce, as he was bidden, and they rode thus a while slowly, Christopher now and then crying, as they went: To the right, squire! To the left! Straight on now! and so on. But suddenly they heard voices, and it was as if the wood had all burst out into fire, so bright a light shone out. Christopher shouted, and hastened on to pass Simon, going quite close to his right side thereby, and as he did so, he saw steel flashing in his

The scorn of Christopher

Simon must needs go on afore

hand, and turned sidling to guard him, but ere he could do aught Simon drave a broad

A felon stroke

dagger into his side, and then turned about and fled the way they had come, so far as he knew how.

New-comers

Christopher fell from his horse at once as the stroke came home, but straightway therewith were there men with torches round about him, a dozen of them; men tall, and wild-looking in the firelight; and one of them, a slim young man with long red hair falling all about his shoulders, knelt down by him, while the others held his horse and gat his feet out of the stirrups. The red-head laid his hand on his breast, and raised his head up till the light of a torch fell on it, and then he cried out: Masters, here hath been a felon; the man hath been sticked, and the deed hath to do with us; for lo you, this is none other than little Christopher of the Uttermost March,

They knew Christopher

who stumbled on the Tofts last Yule, and with whom we were so merry together. Here, thou Robert of Maisey, do thy leechdom on him if he be yet living: but if he be dead, or dieth of his hurt, then do I take the feud on me, to follow it to the utmost against the slayer; even I, David the Red, though I be the youngest of the sons of Jack of the Tofts. For this man I meant should be my fellow in field and fell, ganging and galloping, in hall and high-place, in cot and in choir, before woman and warrior, and priest and proud-prince. Now thou Robert, how does he?

Said the man who had looked to Christopher's wound, and had put aside his coat and shirt: He is sore hurt, but meseemeth not deadly. Nay, belike he may live as long as thou, or longer, whereas thou wilt ever be shoving thy red head and lank body wheresoever knocks are going. David rose with a sigh of one who is lightened of a load, and said: Well Robert, when thou hast bound his wound let us have him unto the house: Ho lads! there is light enough to cut some boughs and make a litter for him. But, ho again! has no one gone after the felon to take him? Robert grinned up from his job with the hurt man: Nay, King David, said he, it is mostly thy business; mayhappen thou wilt lay thy heels on thy neck and after him. The red-head stamped on the ground, and half

drew his sax, and shoved it back again into the sheath, and then said angrily: I marvel at thee, Robert, that thou didst not send a man or two at once after the felon: how may I leave my comrade and sweet board-fellow lying hurt in the wild-wood? Art thou growing over old for our wood-land ways, wherein loitering bringeth louting? Robert chuckled and said: I thought thou wouldst take the fly in thy mouth, foster-son: if the felon escape Ralph Longshanks and Anthony Green, then hath he the devil's luck; and they be after him. That is well, said the young man, though I would I were with them. And therewith he walked up and down impatiently, while the others were getting ready the litter of boughs.

At last it was done, and Christopher laid thereon, and they all went on together through the wood-land path, the torches still flaring about them. Presently they came out into a clearing of the wood, and lo, looming great and black before them against the sky, where the moon had now broken out of the clouds somewhat, the masses of the tofts, and at the top of the northernmost of them a light in the upper window of a tall square tower. Withal, the yellow-litten windows of a long house showed on the plain below the tofts; but little else of the house might be seen, save that, as they drew near, the walls brake out in doubtful light here and there as the torches smote them.

So came they to a deep porch, where they quenched all the torches save one, and entered a great hall through it, David and two other tall young men going first, and Robert Maisey going beside the bier. The said hall was lighted with candles, but not very brightly, save at the upper end; but amidmost a flickering heap of logs sent a thin line of blue smoke up to the luffer. There were some sixty folk in the hall, scattered about the end-long tables, a good few of whom were women, well grown and comely enough, as far as could be seen under the scanty candle-light. At the high-table, withal, were sitting both men and women, and as they drew near to the greater light of it, there could be seen in the chief seat a man, past middle age, tall, wide-shouldered and thin-flanked, with a short peaked beard and close-cut grizzled hair; he was high of cheek bones, thin-faced, with grey eyes, both big and gentle-looking; he was clad in a green coat welted with gold. Beside him sat a woman, tall and big-made, but very fair of face, though she were little younger, belike, than the man. Out from these two sat four men and four women, man by man and woman by woman, on either side of the high-seat. Of the said men, one was of long red hair as David, and like to him in all wise, but older; the others were of like fashion to him in the high-seat. Shortly to say it, his sons they were, as David and the two young men with him. The four women who sat with these men were all fair and young, and one of them, she who drank out of the red-head's cup, so fair, and with such a pleasant

The men in the hall

Women on the dais

slim grace, that her like were not easy to be found.

Again, to shorten the tale, there in the hall before Christopher, who lay unwotting, were Jack of the Tofts and his seven sons, and the four wives of four of the same, whom they had won from the Wailful Castle, when they, with their father, put an end to the evil woman, and the great she-tyrant of the Land betwixt the Wood and the River.

Now when David and his were come up to the dais, they stayed them, and their father spake from his high-seat and said: What is to do, ye three? and what catch have ye? Said David: I would fain hope 'tis the catch of a life that I love; for here is come thy guest of last Yule, even little Christopher, who wrestled with thee and threw thee after thou hadst thrown all of us, and he lying along and hurt, smitten down by a felon hard on our very doors. What will ye do with him?

What, said Jack of the Tofts, but tend him and heal him and cherish him. And when he is well, then we shall see. But where is the felon who smote him? Said David: He fled away a-horseback ere we came to the field of deed, and Anthony Green and Ralph Longshanks are gone after him; and, belike, will take him. Mayhappen not, said the

master. Now, forsooth, I have an inkling
of what this may mean; whereas there can
be but one man whose business may be the
taking of our little guest's life. But let all
be till he be healed and may tell us his tale;
and, if he telleth it as I deem he will, then
shall we seek further tidings. Meanwhile, if
ye take the felon, keep him heedfully till I
may see him; for then may I have a true
tale out of him, even before Christopher is
hale again.

So therewith David and Robert, with two
or three others, brought Christopher to a
chamber, and did what leechdoms to him
they might; but Jack of the Tofts, and his
sons and their fair wives, and his other folk,
made merry in the hall of the Tofts.

The leeching of Christopher

CHAPTER IX. SQUIRE SIMON COMES BACK TO OAKENHAM. THE EARL MARSHAL TAKEN TO KING IN OAKENREALM

Simon gets away

NOW as to Squire Simon, whether the devil helped him, or his luck, or were it his own cunning and his horse's stoutness, we wot not; but in any case he fell not in with Ralph Longshanks and Anthony Green, but rode as far and as fast as his horse would go, and then lay down in the wild-wood; and on the morrow arose and went his ways, and came in the even to the Castle of the Uttermost March, and went on thence the morrow after on a fresh horse to Oakenham. There he made no delay, but went straight to the High House, and had privy speech of the Earl Marshal; and him he told how he had smitten Christopher, and, as he deemed, slain him. The Earl Marshal looked on him grimly and said: Where is the ring, then? I have it not, said Simon. How might I light down to take it, when the seven sons were hard on us? And therewith he told him all the tale, and how he had risen to slay Christopher the even before; and how he had

He comes to Lord Rolf

found out after that the youngling had become guest and fosterling of the folk of the Tofts; and how warily Christopher had ridden, so that he, Simon, had had to do his best at the last moment. And now, Lord, quoth he, I see that it will be my luck to have grudging of thee, or even worse it may be; yea, or thou wilt be presently telling me that I am a liar and never struck the stroke: but I warrant me that by this time Jack of the Tofts knoweth better, for I left my knife in the youngling's breast, and belike he wotteth of my weapons. Well, then, if thou wilt be quit of me, thou hast but to forbear upholding me against the Toft folk, and then am I gone without any to-do of thee.

Simon thinks he has slain Christopher

Earl Rolf spake quietly in answer, though his face was somewhat troubled: Nay, Simon, I doubt thee not, not one word; for why shouldest thou lie to me? nor do I deem thou wouldest, for thou art trusty and worthy. Yet sore I doubt if the child be dead. Well, even so let it be, for I am alive; and full surely I am mightier than Jack of the Tofts, both to uphold thee against him (wherein I shall not fail), and otherwise. But may God make me even as that young man if I be not mightier yet in a few days. But now do thou go and eat and drink and take thy disport; for thou hast served me well; and in a little while I

Rolf gives Simon fair words

Promises are made

shall make thee knight and lord, and do all I can to pleasure thee.

So then Simon knelt to the Earl and made obeisance to him, and arose and went his ways, light-hearted and merry.

A Folk-mote

But within the month it so befel that some of the lords and dukes came to the Earl Marshal, and prayed him to call together a great Folk-mote of all Oakenrealm; and he answered them graciously, and behight them to do as they would; and even so did he. And that Mote was very great, and whenas it was hallowed, there arose a great lord, grey and ancient, and bewailed him before the folk, that they had no king over Oakenrealm to uphold the laws and ward the land; and Will ye live bare and kingless for ever? said he at last. Will ye not choose you a king, and crown him, before I die, and we others of the realm who are old and worn?

Earl Rolf cried on for King

Then he sat down, and another arose, and in plain terms he bade them take the Earl Marshal to king. And then arose one after other, and each sang the same song, till the hearts of the people grew warm with the big words, and at first many, and then more cried out: A King, a King! The Earl Marshal for King! Earl Rolf for King! So that at last the voices rose into a great roar, and sword clashed on shield, and they who were about the Earl turned to him and upraised him on a great war-shield, and he stood thereon above the folk with a naked sword in his hand, and all the folk shouted about him.

Thereafter the chiefs and all the mightiest came and did homage to him for King of Oakenrealm as he sat on the Hill of the Folk-mote: and that night there was once more a King of Oakenrealm, and Earl Rolf was no more, but King Rolf ruled the people.

He is taken to King

But now the tale leaves telling of him, and turns again to Christopher the woodman, who lay sick of his hurt in the House of the Tofts.

CHAPTER X. OF CHRISTOPHER AT THE TOFTS

CHRISTOPHER was six weeks ere he could come and go as he was wont; but it was but a few days ere he was well enough to tell his tale to Jack of the Tofts and his seven bold sons; and they cherished him and made much of him, and so especially did David, the youngest son, to his board-fellow and troth-brother.

On a day, when he was well-nigh whole, as he sat under an oak-tree nigh the house, in the cool of the evening, Jack of the Tofts came to him and sat beside him, and made him tell his tale to him once more, and when he was done he said to him: Foster-son, for so I would have thee deem of thyself, what is the thing that thou rememberest earliest in thy days? Said Christopher: A cot without the Castle walls at the Uttermost Marches, and a kind woman therein, big, sandy-haired, and freckled, and a lad that was white-haired and sturdy, somewhat bigger than I. And I mind me standing up against the door-post of the cot and seeing men-at-arms riding by in white armour, and one of them throwing an apple to me, and I raised my arm to throw it back at him, but my nurse (for somehow I knew she was not my mother) caught my hand and drew me back indoors, and I heard the men laughing behind me. And then a little after my nurse took me into the Castle court, and there was again the man who had thrown me the apple, sitting on a bench therein, clad in a scarlet gown furred with brown fur; and she led me up to him, and he stooped down and chucked me under the chin and put his hand on my head, and looked at my nurse and said: Yea, he is a big lad, and groweth apace, whereas he is but of six winters. Nay, Lord, said my nurse, he is but scantly five. He knit his brows and said: Nay, I tell thee he is six. She shook her head, but said nought, and the great man scowled on her and said: Mistress, wilt thou set thy word against mine? Know now that this child is of six years. Now then, how old is he? She said faintly: Six years. Said he: Look to it that thy head and thy mouth forget it not, else shall we make thy back remember it. Then he put his hand on my head again, and said: Well, I say thou art a big lad for six years; and therewith he gave me a silver penny; and even as he spake, came up a gay-clad squire to him and looked on me curiously. Then I went away with my nurse, and wondered why she was

The child must be of six winters

The nurse is threatened

grown so pale, whereas she was mostly red-cheeked and jolly. But when she had brought me into the cot again, she kissed me and clipped me, weeping sorely the while; wherefore I wept, though I knew not why. Sithence, I soon came to know that the man was the lord and governor of the Castle, as ye may well wot; but to this hour I know not what he meant by threatening my nurse.

Of Christopher's age

Said Jack: And how old art thou now, Christopher mine? Said the youngling, laughing: By my lord the Castellan's reckoning I am twenty and two years; but if thou wilt trow my good and kind nurse, that yet liveth a kind dame, thou must take twelve months off the tale.

Jack sat silent a little; then he laughed and said: Well, thou art a mickle babe, Christopher, and it may be that one day many a man shall know it. But now tell me again; thou hadst said to me before that thou hast known neither father nor mother, brother nor sisters: is it so, verily?

He hath no kindred

Said Christopher: Never a kinsman of blood have I, though many well-wishers. Said Jack: Well, now hast thou father and mother, brethren and sisters, though they be of the sort of man-slayers and strong-thieves and outlaws; yet they love thee, lad, and thou mayst one day find out how far thou mayst trust them.

Christopher nodded and smiled at him merrily; then he fell silent awhile, and the outlaw sat looking on him; at last he said suddenly: *He asks what he is* Foster-father, tell me what I am, and of what kindred, I pray thee; for, methinks, thou knowest thereof; and what wonder, wise man as thou art.

Forsooth, son Christopher, I have a deeming *Jack will have Christopher away* thereof, or somewhat more, and when it is waxen greater yet, I will tell it thee one day, but not now. But hearken! for I have other tidings for thee. Thou art now whole and strong, and in a few days thou mayst wend the wild-wood as stoutly as e'er a one of us. Now, therefore, how sayest thou, if I bid thee fare a two days' journey with David and Gilbert thy brethren, and thy sister Joanna, till they bring thee to a fair little stead which I call mine own, to dwell there awhile? For meseemeth, lad, that the air of the Tofts here may not be over wholesome unto thee.

Christopher reddened, and he half rose up, and said: What is this, foster-father? Is it that there shall be battle at the Tofts, and that thou wouldst have me away thence? Am I then such a weakling?

Said Jack, laughing: Be still now, thou *Jack will so have it* sticked one. The Tofts go down to battle at some whiles; but seldom cometh battle to the Tofts; and no battle do I look for now. But do my bidding, sweet fosterling, and it will be better for me and better for thee, and may, perchance, put off battle for a while; which to me as now were not unhandy. If thou wilt but abide at Littledale for somewhile, there

He shall come back to Yule

shall be going and coming betwixt us, and thou shalt drink thy Yule at the Tofts, and go back afterwards, and ever shalt thou have thy sweet fellows with thee; so be wise, since thou goest not perforce.

Yea, yea, said Christopher, laughing; thou

Come now David and Joanna

puttest force on no man, is it not so, foster-father? Wherefore I will go, and uncompelled.

Therewith came up to them, from out of the wild-wood, David, and with him Joanna, who was the wife of Gilbert, and one of those fair maidens from the Wailful Castle, though not the fairest of them; they had been a-hunting, for ever those three would willingly go together, Gilbert, David, and Joanna; and now Gilbert had abided behind, to dight the quarry for fetching home. Christopher looked on the two joyfully, as a man getting whole after sickness smiles on goodly things; and Joanna was fair to see in her hunter's attire, with brogues tied to her naked feet, and the shapeliness of her legs bare to the knee beneath the trussing up of her green skirts.

Christopher and Joanna

They greeted Christopher kindly, and Joanna sat down by him to talk, but Jack of the Tofts took his son by the arm, and went toward the house with him in earnest speech.

CHAPTER XI. HOW CHRISTOPHER CAME TO LITTLEDALE TO ABIDE THERE A WHILE

IN about a week's time from this, those four fellows went their ways southward from the Tofts, having with them four good nags and four sumpter beasts laden with such things as they needed, whereof were weapons enough, though they all, save Christopher, bare bows; and he and the others were girt with swords, and a leash of good dogs followed them. Two milch kine also they drave with them.

Those four fare their ways

Merry they were all as they went their ways through the woods, but the gladness of Christopher was even past words; wherefore, after a little, he spake scarce at all, but sat in his saddle hearkening the tales and songs and jests of his fellows, who went close beside him, for more often they went a-foot than rode. And, forsooth, as the sweet morning wore, it seemed to him, so great was his joy, as if all the fair show of the greenery, and the boles of the ancient oaks, and the squirrel running from bough to bough, and the rabbits scuttling from under the bracken, and the hind leaping in the woodlawn, and the sun falling through the rustling leaves, and the wind on his face, and the scent

They ride the woodland

The joy of Christopher

of the forest, yea, and his fair companions and their loveliness and valiancy and kindness, and the words and songs that came from their dear mouths, all these seemed to him, as it were, one great show done for the behoof and pleasure of him, the man come from the peril of death and the sick-bed.

Of Little-dale

They lay that night in all glee under the green boughs; and arose on the morrow, and went all day, and again slept in the green-wood, and the next morning came down into a fair valley, which was indeed Littledale, through which ran a pleasant little river; and on a grassy knoll, but a short way from its bank, was a long framed hall, somewhat narrow, and nought high, whitherward they turned them straightway, and were presently before the

They enter the house

door: then Gilbert drew a key from out of his scrip and unlocked the door, and they entered, and found within a fair little hall, with shut-beds out from it on the further side, and kitchen and store-bowers at the end; all things duly appointed with plenishing, and meal and wine; for it was but some three months since one of Jack of the Tofts' allies, Sir Launcelot a' Green and his wife and two bairns, had left it till their affair was made straight; whereas he had dwelt there a whole year, for he had been made an outlaw of Meadham, and was a dear friend of the said Jack.

Now said David smiling: Here is now thine high house and thy castle, little King Christopher; how doth it like thee? Right well, said Christopher; and, to say sooth, I would almost that it were night, or my bones do else, that I might lie naked in a bed.

Nay, lad, said Gilbert, make it night now, and we will do all that needs must be done, while thou liest lazy, as all kings use to do. Nay, said Christopher, I will be more a king than so, for I will do neither this nor that; I will not work and I will not go to bed, but will look on, till it is time for me to take to the crooked stick and the grey-goose wing and seek venison. That is better than well, said David; for I can see by thine eyes, that are dancing with pleasure, that in three or four days thou wilt be about the thickets with us. Meantime, said Joanna, thou shalt pay for thy meat and drink by telling us tales when we come home weary. Yea, said Christopher laughing, that ye may go to sleep before your time.

So they talked, and were joyous and blithe together, and between them they made the house trim, and decked it with boughs and blossoms; and though Christopher told them no tale that night, Joanna and David sang both; and in a night or two it was Christopher that was the minstrel. So when the morrow came there began their life of the wood-land;

Christopher will look on

They are merry

*Yule at
the Tofts*

*Back to
Little-
dale*

but, save for the changing of the year and the chances of the hunt, the time passed on from day to day with little change, and it was but seldom that any man came their way. When Yule was, they locked the house door behind them and went their ways home to the Tofts; and now of all of these wayfarers was Christopher by far the hardest and strongest, for his side had utterly forgotten Simon's knife. At the Tofts they were welcomed with all triumph, and they were about there in the best of cheer, till it was wearing toward Candlemas, and then they took occasion of a bright and sunny day to go back to Littledale once more, and there they abode till spring was come and was wearing into summer, and messages had come and gone betwixt them and the Tofts, and it was agreed that with the first of autumn they should go back to the Tofts and see what should betide. But now leave we Christopher and these good fellows of the Tofts and turn to Goldilind, who is yet dwelling amid no very happy days in the Castle of Greenharbour, on the northernmost marches of Meadham.

CHAPTER XII. OF GOLDILIND IN THE MAY MORNING AT GREEN-HARBOUR

MAY was on the land now, and was come into its second week, and Goldilind awoke on a morn in the Castle of Greenharbour; but little did her eyes behold of the May, even when they were fully open; for she was lying, not in her own chamber, which was proper, and even somewhat stately, and from whence she could look on the sky and green-wood, but in a chamber low down amidst the footings of the wall, little lighted, unadorned, with nought in it for sport or pleasure; nought, forsooth, save the pallet bed on which she lay, a joint stool and water ewer. To be short, though it were called the Least Guard-chamber, it was a prison, and she was there dreeing her penance, as Dame Elinor would call the cruelty of her malice, which the chaplain, Dame Elinor's led captain, had ordained her for some sin which the twain had forged between them.

She lay there naked in her smock, with no raiment anigh her, and this was the third morning whereon she had awakened to the dusky bare walls, and a long while had their

Of Goldilind

A prison

Goldilind lies quiet

emptiness made of the hours: but she lay quiet and musing, not altogether without cheer now; for indeed she was not wont to any longer penance than this she had but now tholed, so she looked for release presently: and, moreover, there had grown in her mind during those three days a certain purpose; to wit, that she would get hold of the governor of the castle privily, and two or three others of the squires who most regarded her, and bewail her case to them, so that she might perchance get some relief. For-

She hath a rede

sooth, as she called to mind this resolve, her heart beat and her cheek flushed, for well she knew that there was peril in it, and she forecast what might be the worst that would come thereof, while, on the other hand, the best that might be seemed to her like a glimpse of Paradise.

A new-comer

As she lay there and turned the matter over in her mind for this many an hundred time, there came a key into the lock, and the door opened; and thereby entered a tall woman, dark-haired, white-skinned, somewhat young, and not ill-favoured: Goldilind still lay there, till the new-comer said to her in a hard voice, wherein was both threatening and mockery:

Of Aloyse

Rise up, our Lady! the Dame Elinor saith that it is enough, and that thou art to go forth. Nay, hold a while; for I say unto thee that it is yet early in the day, and that thy chamber is not yet dight for thee, so thou must needs bestow thyself elsewhere till it be done. Goldilind rose up, and said smiling: Yea, Aloyse, but thou hast not brought my raiment: and thou seest! The maid stood looking at her a moment somewhat evilly, and then said: Well, since it is but scant six o'clock, I may do that; but I bid thee ask me not overmuch; for meseemeth Dame Elinor is not overwell pleased with thee to-day, nor our chaplain either. Therewith she turned and went out, locking the door behind her, and came back presently bearing on her arm a green gown *Raiment* and other raiment: she laid them on the stool *is* before the Lady, and said: Hasten, my Lady, *brought* and let me go to my place: sooth to say, it may well be double trouble to thee to don thy clothes, for thou mayst have to doff them again before long.

Goldilind answered nought, but reddened and *They* paled again as she clad her under the waiting *come out* maid's eyes. Then they went out together, *of the* and up a short stone stair, till they were level *prison* with the greensward without. Then the maid turned to Goldilind and said: And now thou art clad and out, my Lady, I wot not where thou art to go to, since to thy chamber thou must not go. Nay, hold and hearken! here we be at the door which opens on to the Foresters' Garth under the Foresters' Tower, thither shalt thou abide till I come to fetch thee.   How now, my Lady! what else wouldst thou?   Goldilind

Goldilind craves bread

looked on her with a smile, yet with eager eyes, and said: O good Aloyse, wouldst thou but give me a piece of bread? for I hunger; thou wottest my queenly board hath not been overloaded these last days.   Ha! said Aloyse; if thou ask me overmuch I fear thou mayst pay for it, my Lady; but this last asking thou shalt have, and then none other till all thy penance thou hast dreed.   Abide!

Aloyse gives it her in the garden

Therewith she went up the stairs, and Goldilind, who now was but weak with her prison and the sudden light, and the hope and fear of her purpose of bewailing her story, sat her down on the stair there, almost, as it were, 'twixt home and hell, till her heart came back to her and the tears began to flow from her eyes.   Forthright came back Aloyse, bearing a white loaf and a little pitcher of milk on a silver serving-dish; she laid them down, unlocked the door into the garden, and thrust Goldilind through by the shoulders; then she turned and took up her serving-dish with the bread and milk, and handed it to Goldilind through the door, and said: Now is my Lady served.   It were indeed well that my Lady should strengthen herself this hour for the hour next to come. Therewith she turned about, and shut and locked the door; and the King's daughter fell to eagerly on her bread, and thought of little till she had eaten and drunk, save that she felt the sweet scent of the gilliflowers and eglantine as it were a part of her meal.

Goldilind eats

Then she went slowly down the garden, treading the greensward beside the flowers; and she looked on the hold, and the low sun gilded the walls thereof and glittered in a window here and there, and though there was on her a foreboding of the hours of that day, she did what she might to make the best of the fragrant May morning and the song of birds and rustle of leaves, though, indeed, at whiles the tears would gush out of her eyes when she thought how young she was and how 'feeble, and the pity of herself became sweet unto her.

She weeps withal

CHAPTER XIII. OF GOLDILIND IN THE GARTH

*Comes
a mes-
senger*

NOW, as she went in that garden with her face turned toward the postern which led into the open space of the green-wood, which was but two bow-shots from the thicket, she heard the clatter of horse-hoofs on the loose stones of the path, and how they stopped at the said postern; and presently there was a key in the lock, the door opened, and a man came in walking stiffly, like a rider who has ridden far and fast. He was clad in jack and sallet, and had a sword by his side, and on his sleeve was done in green and gold a mountain aflame; so that Goldilind knew him at once for a man of Earl Geoffrey's; and, indeed, she had seen the man before, coming and going on errands that she knew nought of, and on which nothing followed that was of import to her. Therefore, as she watched him cross the garden and go straight up to the door of the Foresters' Tower, and take out another key and enter, she heeded him but little, nor did his coming increase her trouble a whit.

*An open
door*

She walked on toward the postern, and now she saw that the errand-bearer had left it open behind him, and when she came close up to it, she saw his horse tied to a ring in the wall, a strong and good bay nag. The sight of him, and the glimpse of the free and open land, stirred in her the misery of her days and the yearning for the loveliness of the world without, converse of friends, hope of the sufficiency of desire, and the sweetness of love returned. And so strong a wave of anguish swept over her, that she bowed her down upon the grass and wept bitterly. Yet but a little while it lasted; she rose up presently and looked warily all round her, and up to the Castle, and saw none stirring; she drew up the skirts of her green gown into her girdle, till the hem but just hid her knees; then she stepped lightly through the half-open door with flushed cheeks and glittering eyes, while her heart rose within her; then she lifted her hand, unhitched the reins from the iron ring, and quietly led the horse close under the garth-wall, and stole gently up the slope which, as all roads from the Castle, went straightway toward the thicket, but this was the straightest. So she went, till she came to the corner of the garth-wall, and a little further; and the Castle on that side was blind, save for the swale on the battlement, whereon in that deep peace was little going: and, moreover, it was not even yet six o'clock.

A purpose in Goldilind

She goeth out a-gate

CHAPTER XIV.   GOLDILIND GOES FREE

THERE then she stayed the horse, and, flushed and panting, got lightly into the saddle and bestrode it, and, leaning forward on the beast's neck, smote his flanks with her heels; the horse was fresh, though his master had been weary, whereas the said messenger had gotten him from a forester some six miles away in the wood that morning, so the nag answered to her call for speed, and she went a great gallop into the wood, and was hidden in a twinkling from any eyes that might be looking out of the Castle.

Without checking the nag she sped along, half mad with joy at the freedom of this happy morn.   Nigh aimless she was, but had an inkling that it were well with her if she could hold northward ever; for the old man aforesaid had told her of Oakenrealm, and how it lay northward of them; so that way she drifted as the thicket would suffer her.   When she had gone as much of a gallop as she might for some half hour, she drew rein to breathe her nag, and hearkened; she turned in the saddle, but heard nought to affright her, so she went on again, but somewhat more soberly; and thus-wise she rode for some two hours, and the day waxed hot, and she was come to a clear pool amidst of a little clearing, covered with fine greensward right down to the water's edge.

There she made stay, and got off her horse, and stood awhile by him as he cropped the sweet grass; and the birds sang at the edge of the thicket, and the rabbits crept and gambolled on the other side of the water; and from the pool's edge the moorhens cried. She stood half leaning against the side of the horse till she became somewhat drowsy; yea, and even dreamed a little, and that little but ill, it seemed, as she gave a troubled cry and shrank together and turned pale. Then she rubbed her eyes and smiled, and turned to the pool, where now a little ripple was running over the face of it, and a thought came upon her, and she set her hand to the clasp of her gown and undid it, and drew the gown off her shoulders, and so did off all her raiment, and stood naked a little on the warm sunny grass, and then bestirred her and went lightly into the pool, and bathed and sported there, and then came on to the grass again, and went to and fro to dry her in the air and sun. Then she did on her raiment again, and laid her down under a thorn-bush by the pool-side, and there, would she, would she not, went to sleep soundly, and dreamed not. And when she awoke she

She stayeth

She noteth the water

Of Goldilind's bathing

deemed her sleep had been long, but it was not
so, but scarce a score of minutes. Anyhow,
she sprang up now and went to her horse, and
drew the girths tight (which she had loosed
erewhile), and so bestrode the good horse,
and shook the reins, and rode away much
comforted and enhearted.

CHAPTER XV. OF GOLDILIND IN THE WILD-WOOD

GOLDILIND rode on, hastening yet to put as many miles as she might betwixt her and Greenharbour. Within a three hours from her bathing she fell a-hungering sore, and knew not what to do to eat, till she found a pouch made fast to the saddle-bow, and therein a little white loaf, that and no more, which she took and ate the half of with great joy, sitting down by a brook-side, whence she had her drink.

Goldilind findeth bread

Then again she mounted, and rode on till dusk overtook her just as she came to a little river running from the north from pool to shallow, and shallow to pool. And whereas she was now exceeding weary, and the good horse also much spent, and that the grass was very sweet and soft down to the water's edge, and that there was a thick thorn-bush to cover her, she made up her mind that this place should be her bedchamber. So she took saddle and bridle off the horse, as he must needs bite the grass, and then when she had eaten the other half of her bread, she laid her down on the green grass with her head on the

*She
sleeps a
night-
tide*

saddle, and when she had lain listening to the horse cropping the grass close anigh her for a minute or two, she fell fast asleep, and lay there long and had no dreams.

CHAPTER XVI. WHAT GOLDILIND FOUND IN THE WOOD

WHEN she awoke it was broad day and bright sun, and she rose up to her feet and looked about, and saw the horse standing close by, and sharing the shade with her, whisking his tail about lazily. Then she turned, and saw the stream rippling out from the pool over the clean gravel, and here and there a fish darting through the ripple, or making clean rings on the pool as he quietly took a fly; the sky was blue and clear, there was scarce a breath of air, and the morning was already hot; no worse than yesterday sang the birds in the bushes; but as she looked across the river, where, forsooth, the alders grew thick about the pool's edge, a cock blackbird, and then another, flew out from the close boughs, where they had been singing to their mates, with the sharp cry that they use when they are frighted. Withal she saw the bush move, though, as aforesaid, the morning was without wind. She had just stooped to do off her foot-gear (for she was minded to bathe again), but now she stopped with one shoe in her hand, and looked on the bushes keenly with beating heart, and

Her waking

Fowl by the river

*Goldilind
espies
the bank*

again she thought she saw the boughs shaken, and stood, not daring to move a while; but they moved no more now when she had looked steadily at them a space, and again a blackbird began singing loud just where they had been shaken. So she gathered heart again, and presently turned her hand once more to stripping her raiment off her, for she would not be baulked of her bath; but when the stripping was done, she loitered not naked on the bank as she had done the day before, but walked swiftly into the shallow, and thence down into the pool, till nothing but her head and the whiteness of her shoulders showed over the dark water. Even then she turned her head about twice or thrice to look into the over-side bushes, but when she saw nothing stir there she began to play in the water, but not for long, but came splashing through the shallow and hurried on her raiment.

*Of her
bath*

*She fords
the river.*

When she was clad again she went up to the horse, and patted and caressed him, and did bridle and saddle on him, and was going to climb upon him, when, of a sudden, she thought she would lead him across, lest there should be a hole near the other bank and he might stumble into it unwarily; so she bared her feet once more and trussed up her gown skirts, and so took the ford, leading the beast; the water was nowhere up to mid-leg of her, and she stepped ashore on to short and fine grass, which spread like a meadow before her, with a big thorn or two scattered about it, and a little grassy hill beset with tall elms toward the top, coming down into the flat of the meadow and drawing round it nearly up to the river on the north side.

New tidings

But now she stood staring in wonder and some deal of fear; for there were three milch kine feeding on the meadow, and, moreover, under a thorn, scarce a hundred yards from where she stood, was a tall man standing gazing on her. So stricken was she that she might neither cry out nor turn aside; neither did she think to pull her gown out of her girdle to cover the nakedness of her legs.

A man in the mead

When they had thus stood a little while the man began to move toward her very slowly, nor did she dare to flee any the more. But when he was within half a dozen paces her face flushed red, and she did pull her gown out of its trusses and let it flow down. But he spake to her in a pleasant voice, and said: May I speak to thee, maiden? Fear was yet in her soul, so that she might not speak for a little, and then she said: O, I beseech thee, bring me not back to Greenharbour! And she paled sorely as she spake the word. But he said: I wot not of Greenharbour, how to find the way thereto, though we have heard of

He speaketh

it. But comfort thyself, I pray thee, there is nought to fear in me.

The sound of his voice was full pleasant to her, and when she hearkened him, how kind and frank it was, then she knew how much of terror was blent with her joy in her newly-won freedom and the delight of the kind and happy words. Yet still she spoke not, and was both shamefast and still not altogether unafraid. Yet, sooth to say, though his attire was but simple, he was nought wild or fierce to look on. From time to time she looked on him, and then dropped her eyes again. In those glances she saw that he was grey-eyed, and smooth-cheeked, and round-chinned, and his hair curly and golden; and she must needs think that she had never seen any face half so fair. He was clad but in a green coat that came not down to his knees, and brogues were tied to his feet, and no more raiment he had; and for hat he had made him a garland of white may blossom, and well it sat there: and again she looked on him, and thought him no worse than the running angel that goes before the throne of God in the picture of the choir of Meadhamstead; and she looked on him and marvelled.

Now she hung her head before him and wished he would speak, and even so did he, and said: Maiden, when I first saw thee from amidst of the bush by the river yonder, I deemed thou wert a wood-wight, or some one of the she-Gods of the Gentiles come back hither. For this is a lonely place, and some deem that the Devil hath might here more than in other places; and when I saw thee, that thou wouldst do off thy raiment to bathe thee, though soothly I longed to lie hidden there, I feared thee, lest thou shouldst be angry with me if I were to see thee unclad; so I came away; yet I went not far, for I was above all things yearning to see thee; and sooth it is, that hadst thou not crossed the water, I should presently have crossed it myself to seek thee, wert thou Goddess, or wood-wife, or whatever might have come of it. But now thou art come to us, and I have heard thy voice beseeching me not to bring thee to Greenharbour, I see that thou art a woman of the kindred of Adam. And yet so it is, that even now I fear thee somewhat. Yet I will pray thee not to be wroth if I ask thee whether I may do aught for thy need. *He tells of how he would see her*

Now she began somewhat to smile, and she looked him full in the face, and said: Forsooth, my need is simple, for I am hungry. He smote himself on the breast, and said: See now, what a great fool I am, not to have known it without telling, instead of making long-winded talk about myself. Come quickly, dear maiden, *He prays her mercy*

She will have victual

and leave thine horse to crop the grass. So
he hurried on to the thorn-bush aforesaid, and
she went foot to foot with him, but he touched
her not; and straightway she sat her down on
the root of the thorn, and smiled frankly on
him, and said:

Nay, sir, and now thou hast made me go all
this way I am out of breath and weary, so I
pray thee of the victual at once. But he had
been busy with his scrip which he had left cast
down there, and therewithal reached out to her
a mighty hunch of bread and a piece of white
cheese, and said:

Now shall I fetch thee milk. Wherewith he
took up a bowl of aspen tree that had lain by
the scrip, and ran off to one of the kine and
milked the bowl full, and came back with it
heedfully, and set it down beside her, and said:
This was the nighest thing to hand, but when
thou hast eaten and rested then shall we go to
our house, if thou wilt be so kind to me; for
there have we better meat, and wine to boot.

She looked up at him smiling, but her
pleasure of the meat and the kindness was so
exceeding, that she might not refrain from
tears also, but she spake not. As for him, he
knelt beside her, looking on her wistfully; and
at last he said: I shall tell thee, that I am glad
that thou wert hungry and that I have seen
thee eating, else might I have deemed thee

somewhat other than a woman of mankind even yet. She said: Yea, and why wouldst thou not believe my word thereto? He said, reddening: I almost fear to tell thee, lest thou think me over bold and be angry with me. Nay, she said, tell me, for I would know. Said he: The words are not easy in my rude mouth; but this is what I mean: that though I be young I have seen fair women not a few, but beside any of them thou art a wonder; . . . and loth I were if thou wert not really of mankind, if it were but for the glory of the world.

He praises her fairness

She hung her head and answered nought a while, and he also seemed ashamed: but presently she spake: Thou hast been kind to us, wouldst thou tell us thy name? and then, if it like thee, what thou art?

Lady, he said, my name is easy to tell, I hight Christopher; and whiles folk in merry mockery call me Christopher King; meseems because I am of the least account of all carles. As for what else I am, a woodman I am, an outlaw and the friend of them: yet I tell thee I have never by my will done any harm to any child of man; and those friends of mine, who are outlaws also, are kind and loving with me, both man and woman, though needs must they dwell aloof from kings' courts and barons' halls. She looked at him wondering, and as if she did not altogether understand him; and she said:

His name

*Of his
dwelling
and
friends*

Where dost thou dwell? He said: To-day I dwell hard by; though where I shall dwell to-morrow, who knows. And with me are dwelling three of my kind fellows; and the dearest is a young man of mine own age, who is my fellow in all matters, for us to live and die each for the other. Couldst thou have seen him, thou wouldst love him I deem. What name hath he? said Goldilind. He hight David, said Christopher.

*She will
not tell of
her name*

But therewith he fell silent and knit his brow, as though he were thinking of some knotty point: but in a while his face cleared, and he said: If I durst, I would ask thee thy name, and what thou art? As to my name, said she, I will not tell it thee as now. As to what I am, I am a poor prisoner; and much have I been grieved and tormented, so that my body hath been but a thing whereby I might suffer anguish. Something else am I, but I may not tell thee what as yet.

*He tells
of a
thought*

He looked on her long, and then arose and went his way along the very track of their footsteps, and he took the horse and brought him back to the thorn, and stood by the lady and reddened, and said: I must tell thee what I have been doing these last minutes. Yea, said she, looking at him wonderingly, hast thou not been fetching my horse to me? So it is, said he; but something else also. Ask me, or

I cannot tell thee. She laughed and said: What else, fair sir? Said he: Ask me what, or I cannot tell thee. Well, what, then? said she. He answered, stammering and blushing: *He tells what it was* I have been looking at thy footprints, whereby thou camest up from the water, to see what new and fairer blossoms have come up in the meadow where thy feet were set e'en now. She answered him nothing, and he held his peace. But in a while she said: If thou wouldst have us come to thine house, thou shalt lead us thither now. And therewith she took her foot-gear from out of her girdle, as if she would do it on, and he turned his face away, but sighed therewith. Then she reddened and put them back again, and rose up lightly, and said: I will go afoot; and wilt thou lead the horse for me?

So did he, and led her by all the softest and most flowery ways, turning about the end of a spur of the little hill that came close to the water, and going close to the lip of the river. And when they had thus turned about the hill there was a somewhat wider vale before them, grassy and fair, and on a knoll, not far from the water, a long frame-house thatched with reed. Then said Christopher: Lady, this is now Littledale, and yonder the house thereof. She said quietly: Lovely is the dale, and fair the house by seeming, and I would that they

They walk onward

They come to Littledale

may be happy that dwell therein! Said Christopher: Wilt thou not speak that blessing within the house as without? Fain were I thereof, she said. And therewith they came into the garth, wherein the apple trees were blossoming, and Goldilind spread abroad her hands and lifted up her head for joy of the sight and the scent, and they stayed awhile before they went on to the door, which was half open, for they feared none in that place, and looked for none whom they might not deal with if he came as a foe.

Christopher would have taken a hand of her to lead her in, but both hands were in her gown to lift up the hem as she passed over the threshold; so he durst not.

Of the house within

Fair and bright now was the hall within, with its long and low windows goodly glazed, a green halling on the walls of Adam and Eve and the garden, and the good God walking therein; the sun shone bright through the southern windows, and about the porch it was hot, but further toward the dais cool and pleasant.

They dine in the hall

So Goldilind sat down in the coolest of the place at the standing table; but Christopher bestirred himself, and brought wine and white bread, and venison and honey, and said: I pray thee to dine, maiden, for it is now hard on noon; and as for my fair fellows, I look not for them before sunset, for they were going far into the wood. She smiled on him, and ate and drank a little deal, and he with her. Sooth to say, her heart was full, and though she had forgotten her fear, she was troubled, because, for as glad as she was, she could not be as glad as her gladness would have her, for the sake of some lack, she knew not what.

Now spake Christopher: I would tell thee *Chris-* something strange, to wit, though it is little *topher* more than three hours since I first saw thee *speaks* beside the river, yet I seem to know thee as if thou wert a part of my life. She looked on him shyly, and he went on: This also is strange, and, withal, it likes me not, that when I speak of my fair fellows here, David, and Gilbert, and Joanna, they are half forgotten to my heart, though their names are on my tongue; and this house, doth it like thee, fair guest? Yea, much, she said; it seems joyous *She an-* to me: and I shall tell thee that I have mostly *swereth* dwelt in unmerry houses, though they were of greater cost than this. Said Christopher: To me it hath been merry and happy enough; but now it seems to me as if it had all been made for thee and this meeting. Is it therefore no longer merry to thee because of that? she said, smiling, yet flushing much red therewith. Now it was his turn not to answer her, and she cast down her eyes before him, and there was silence between them.

*She
asketh a
question*

Then she looked at him steadily, and said: It is indeed grievous that thou shouldest forget thine old friends for me, and that it should have come into thy mind that this fair and merry house was not made for thy fair fellows and thy delight with them, but for me, the chance-comer. For hearken, whereas thou saidst e'en now, that I was become a part of thy life, how can that be? For if I become the poor captive again, how canst thou get to me, thou who art thyself a castaway, as thou hast told me? Yea, but even so, I shall be too low for thee to come down to me. And if I become what I should be, then I must tell thee that I shall be too high for thee to climb up to me; so that in one way or other we shall be sundered, who have but met for an hour or two.

*She
warns
him*

He hung his head a while as they stood there face to face, for both of them had arisen from the board; but presently he looked up to her with glittering eyes, and said: Yea, for an hour or two; why then do we tarry and linger, and say what we have no will to say, and refrain from what our hearts bid us?

*He is
eager*

Therewith he caught hold of her right wrist, and laid his hand on her left shoulder, and this first time that he had touched her, it was as if a fire ran through all his body and changed it into the essence of her: neither was there any naysay in her eyes, nor any defence against him in the yielding body of her.   But even in that nick of time he drew back a little, and turned his head, as a man listening, toward the door, and said: Hist! hist! Dost thou hear, maiden?   She turned deadly pale: O what is it? What is it?   Yea, I hear; it is horses drawing nigh, and the sound of hounds baying.   But may it not be thy fellows coming back?   Nay, nay, he said; they rode not in armour.   Hark to it! and these hounds are deep-voiced sleuth-dogs!   But come now, there may yet be time.

Now come folk thither

He turned, and caught up axe and shield from off the wall, and drew her toward a window that looked to the north, and peered out of it warily; but turned back straightway, and said: Nay, it is too late that way, they are all round about the house.   Maiden, get thou up into the solar by this stair, and thou wilt find hiding-place behind the traverse of the bed; and if they go away, and my fellows come in due time, then art thou safe.   But if not, surely they shall do thee no hurt; for I think, indeed, that thou art some great one.

They are compassed about

And he fell to striding down the hall toward the door; but she ran after him, and caught his arm, and said: Nay, nay, I will not hide, to be dragged out of my refuge like a thief: thou sayest well that I am of the great; I will stand by thee and command and forbid as a Queen. O go not to the door!   Stay by me, stay!

Christopher sets on

*They
enter
the hall*

Nay, nay, he said, there is nought for it but the deed of arms. Look! seest thou not steel by the porch? And therewith he broke from her and ran to the door, and was met on the very threshold by all-armed men, upon whom he fell without more ado, crying out: For the Tofts! For the Tofts! The woodman to the rescue! And he hewed right and left on whatsoever was before him, so that what fell not, gave back, and for a moment of time he cleared the porch; but in that nick of time his axe brake on the basnet of a huge man-at-arms, and they all thrust them on him together and drave him back into the hall, and came bundling after him in a heap. But he drave his shield at one, and then with his right hand smote another on the bare face, so that he rolled over and stirred no more till the day of doom. Then was there a weapon before him, might he have stooped to pick it up; but he might not; so he caught hold of a sturdy but somewhat short man by the collar and the lap of his leather surcoat, and drew aback, and with a mighty heave cast him on the route of them,

*Chris-
topher's
stout
defence*

who for their parts had drawn back a little also, as if he had been a huge stone, and down went two before that artillery; and they set up a great roar of wonder and fear. But he followed them, and this time got an axe in his hand, so mazed they were by his onset, and he hewed at them again and drave them aback to the threshold of the door; but could get them no further, and they began to handle long spears to thrust at him.

But then came forward a knight, no mickle man, but clad in very goodly armour, with a lion beaten in gold on his green surcoat; this man smote up the spears, and made the men go back a little, while he stood on the threshold: so Christopher saw that he would parley with him, and forebore him, and the knight spake: Thou youngling, art thou mad? What doest thou falling on my folk? And what do ye, said Christopher fiercely, besetting the houses of folk with weapons? Now wilt thou take my life. But I shall yet slay one or two before I die. Get thee back, lord, or thou shalt be the first. *A knight would hold parley*

But the knight, who had no weapon in his hand, said: We come but to seek our own, and that is our Lady of Meadham, who dwelleth at Greenharbour by her own will. And if thou wilt stand aside thou mayst go free to the devil for us. *He claims Goldilind*

Now would Christopher have shouted and fallen on, and gone to his death there and then; but even therewith a voice, clear and sweet, spake at the back of him, and said: Thou kind host, do thou stand aside and let us speak that which is needful. And therewith stepped forth *Goldilind speaketh*

Goldilind and stood beside Christopher, and said: Sir Burgreve, we rode forth to drink the air yesterday, and went astray amidst the wild-wood, and were belated, so that we must needs lie down under the bare heaven; but this morning we happened on this kind forester, who gave us to eat, and took us to his house and gave us meat and drink; for which it were seemlier to reward him than threaten him. Now it is our pleasure that ye lead us back to Greenharbour; but as for this youth, that ye do him no hurt; but let him go free, according to thy word spoken e'en now, Sir Burgreve.

Speaketh the Bur-greve

She spake slowly and heavily, as one who hath a lesson to say, and it was to be seen of her that all grief was in her heart, though her words were queenly. Some of them that heard laughed; but the Burgreve spake, and said: Lady, we will do thy will in part, for we will lead thee to Greenharbour in all honour; but

Chris-topher yields him

as to this young man, if he will not be slain here and now, needs must he with us. For he hath slain two of our men outright, and hath hurt many, and, methinks, the devil of the woods is in his body. So do thou bid him be quiet, if thou wouldst not see his blood flow.

She turned a pale unhappy face on Christopher, and said: My friend, we bid thee withstand them no more, but let them do with thee as they will.

Christopher stood aside therewith, and sat down on a bench and laughed, and said in a high voice: Stout men-at-arms, forsooth, to take a maid's kirtle to their shield. But therewith the armed men poured into the hall, and a half dozen of the stoutest came up unto Christopher where he sat, and bound his hands with their girdles, and he withstood them no whit, but sat laughing in their faces, and made as if it were all a Yule-tide game. But inwardly his heart burned with anger, and with love of that sweet Lady.

Then they made him stand up, and led him without the house, and set him on a horse, and linked his feet together under the belly thereof. And when that was done he saw them lead out the Lady, and they set her in a horse litter, and then the whole troop rode off together, with two men riding on either side of the said litter. In this wise they left Littledale.

They bind him

They depart with the twain

CHAPTER XVII. GOLDILIND COMES BACK TO GREENHARBOUR.

THEY rode speedily, and had with them men who knew the wood-land ways, so that the journey was nought so long thence as Goldilind had made it thither; and they stayed not for nightfall, since the moon was bright, so that they came before the Castle-gate before midnight. Now Goldilind looked to be cast into prison, whatever might befall her upon the morrow; but so it went not, for she was led straight to her own chamber, and one of her women, but not Aloyse, waited on her, and when she tried to have some tidings of her, the woman spake to her no more than if she were dumb. So

all unhappily she laid her down in her bed, foreboding the worst, which she deemed might well be death at the hand of her jailers. As for Christopher, she saw the last of him as they entered the Castle-gate, and knew not what they had done with him. So she lay in dismal thoughts, but at last fell asleep for mere weariness.

When she awoke it was broad day, and there was someone going about in the chamber; she turned, and saw that it was Aloyse. She felt

sick at heart, and durst not move or ask of
tidings; but presently Aloyse turned, and came
to the bed, and made an obeisance, but spake not.
Goldilind raised her head, and said wearily:
What is to be done, Aloyse, wilt thou tell me?
For my heart fails me, and, meseems, unless
they have some mercy, I shall die to-day. Nay,
said the chambermaid, keep thine heart up; for
here is one at hand who would see thee, when
it is thy pleasure to be seen. Yea, said Goldilind, Dame Elinor to wit. And she moaned,
and fear and heart-sickness lay so heavy on her
that she went nigh to swooning.

But Aloyse lifted up her head, and brought
her wine and made her drink, and when Goldilind was come to herself again the maid said:
I say, keep up thine heart, for it is not Dame
Elinor and the rods that would see thee, but a
mighty man; nay, the most mighty, to wit,
Earl Geoffrey, who is King of Meadham in all
but the name. Goldilind did in sooth take
heart at this tidings, and she said: I wonder
what he may have to do here; all this while he
hath not been to Greenharbour, or, mayhappen,
it might have been better for me. I wot not,
said Aloyse, but even so it is. I shall tell thee,
the messenger, whose horse thou didst steal,
brought no other word in his mouth save this,
that my Lord Earl was coming; and come he
did; but that was toward sunset, long after

*Now
comes
to her
Aloyse*

*Aloyse
tells
tidings*

*Of Earl
Geoffrey*

they had laid the blood-hounds on thy slot, and I had been whipped for letting thee find the way out a-gates. Now, our Lady, when thou hast seen the Earl, and hast become our Lady and Mistress indeed, wilt thou bethink thee of the morn before yesterday on my behalf? Yea, said Goldilind, if ever it shall befall. Befall it shall, said Aloyse; I dreamed of thee three nights ago, and thou sitting on thy throne commanding and forbidding the great men. But at worst no harm hath happened, save to my shoulders and sides, by thy stealing thyself, since thou hast come back in the nick of time, and of thine own will, as men say. But tell me now of thine holiday, and if it were pleasant to thee.

Goldilind fell a-weeping at the word, bethinking her of yesterday morning, and Aloyse stood looking on her, but saying nought. At last spake Goldilind softly: Tell me, Aloyse, didst thou hear any speaking of that young man who was brought in hither last night? Have they slain him? Said Aloyse: Soothly, my Lady, I deem they have done him no hurt, though I wot not for sure. There hath been none headed or hanged in the base-court to-day. I heard talk amongst the men-at-arms of one whom they took; they said he was a wonder of sheer strength, and how that he cast their men about as though he were playing at ball.

Aloyse bids a boon

Goldilind asks of Christopher

Aloyse tells of him

Sooth to say, they seemed to bear him no grudge therefor. But now I would counsel thee to arise; and I am bidden to tire and array thee at the best. And now I would say a word in thine ear, to wit, that Dame Elinor feareth thee somewhat this morn.

So Goldilind arose, and was arrayed like a very queen, and was served of what she would by Aloyse and the other women, and sat in her chamber a-waiting the coming of the mighty Lord of Meadham.

Now comes Earl Geoffrey

CHAPTER XVIII. EARL GEOFFREY SPEAKS WITH GOLDILIND

BUT a little while had she sat there, before footsteps a many came to the door, which was thrown open, and straight it was as if the sun had shone on a flower-bed, for there was come Earl Geoffrey and his lords all arrayed most gloriously. Then came the Earl up the chamber to Goldilind, and bent the knee before her, and said: Lady and Queen, is it thy pleasure that thy servant should kiss thine hand? She made him little cheer, but reached out to him her lily hand in its gold sleeve, and said: Thou must do thy will. So he kissed the hand reverently, and said: And these my lords, may they enter and do obeisance and kiss hands, my Lady? Said Goldilind: I will not strive to gainsay their will, or thine, my Lord.

So they entered and knelt before her, and kissed her hand; and, to say sooth, most of them had been fain to kiss both hands of her, yea, and her cheeks and her lips; though but little cheer she made them, but looked sternly on them. Then the Earl spake to her, and told her of her realm, and how folk thrived, and of the deep peace that was upon the land, and of the merry days of Meadham, and the

He does obeisance to her

He speaks with Goldilind

praise of the people. And she answered him
nothing, but as he spake her bosom began to
heave, and the tears came into her eyes and
rolled down her cheeks. Then man looked on
man, and the Earl said: My masters, I deem
that my Lady hath will to speak to me privily,
as to one who is her chiefest friend and well-
willer. Is it so, my Lady? She might not
speak for the tears that welled out from her
heart; but she bowed her head and strove to
smile on him.

*The Earl
is alone
with
Goldilind*

But the Earl waved his hand, and those
lords, and the women also, voided the chamber,
and left those two alone, the Earl standing
before her. But ere he could speak, she arose
from her throne and fell on her knees before
him, and joined hands palm to palm, and cried
in a broken voice: Mercy! Mercy! Have pity
on my young life, great Lord! But he lifted
her up, and set her on her throne again, and
said: Nay, my Lady, this is unmeet; but if
thou wouldst talk and tell with me I am ready to
hearken. She strove with her passion a while,
and then she said: Great Lord, I pray thee to
hearken, and to have patience with a woman's
weak heart. Prithee, sit down here beside me.
It were unfitting, he said; I shall take a lowlier
seat. Then he drew a stool to him, and sat
down before her, and said: What aileth thee?
What wouldest thou?

*She
prayeth
mercy
of him*

*She tells
of her
prison*

Then she said: Lord Earl, I am in prison; I would be free. Quoth he: Yea, and is this a prison then? Yea, she said, since I may not so much as go out from it and come back again unthreatened; yet have I been, and that unseldom, in a worser prison than this: do thou go look on the Least Guard-chamber, and see if it be a meet dwelling for thy master's daughter.

*He
wonders
at her
beauty*

He spake nought awhile; then he said: And yet, if it grieveth thee, it marreth thee nought; for when I look on thee mine eyes behold the beauty of the world, and the body wherein is no lack. She reddened and said: If it be so, it is God's work, and I praise him therefore. But how long will it last? For grief slayeth beauty.

He looked on her long, and said: To thy friends I betook thee, and I looked that they should cherish thee; where then is the wrong that I have done thee? She said: Maybe no wrong wittingly; since now, belike, thou art come to tell me that all this weary sojourn is at an end, and that thou wilt take me to Mead-hamstead, and set me on the throne there, and show my father's daughter to all the people.

*He
nay-says
her
asking*

He held his peace, and his face grew dark before her while she watched it. At last he spake in a harsh voice: Lady, he said, it may not be; here in Greenharbour must thou abide, or in some other castle apart from the folk. Yea, she said, now I see it is true, that which I foreboded when first I came hither: thou wouldst slay me, that thou mayest sit safely in the seat of thy master's daughter; thou durst not send me a man with a sword to thrust me through, therefore thou hast cast me into prison amongst cruel jailers, who have been bidden by thee to take my life slowly and with torments. Hitherto I have withstood their malice and thine; but now am I overcome, and since I know that I must die, I have now no fear, and this is why I am bold to tell thee this that I have spoken, though I wot now I shall be presently slain. And now I tell thee I repent it, that I have asked grace of a graceless face.

She is wroth with him

Although she spake strong words, it was with a mild and steady voice. But the Earl was sore troubled, and he rose up and walked to and fro of the chamber, half drawing his sword and thrusting it back into the scabbard from time to time. At last he came back to her, and sat down before her, and spake:

The Earl is troubled

Maiden, thou art somewhat in error. True it is that I would sit firm in my seat and rule the land of Meadham, as belike none other could. True it is also that I would have thee, the rightful heir, dwell apart from the turmoil for a while at least; for I would not have thy white hands thrust me untimely from my place,

He will not have her undo him

or thy fair face held up as a banner by my foemen. Yet nowise have I willed thy death or thine anguish; and if all be true as thou sayest it, and thou art so lovely that I know not how to doubt it, tell me then what these have done with thee.

She said: Sir, those friends to whom thou hast delivered me are my foes, whether they were thy friends or not. Wilt thou compel me to tell thee all my shame? They have treated me as a thrall who had whiles to play a queen's part in a show. To wit, thy chaplain whom thou hast given me has looked on me with lustful eyes, and has bidden me buy of him ease and surcease of pain with my very body, and hath threatened me more evil else, and kept his behest.

Then leapt up the Earl and cried out: Hah! did he so? Then I tell thee his monk's hood shall not be stout enough to save his neck. Now, my child, thou speakest; tell me more, since my hair is whitening.

She said: The sleek, smooth-spoken woman to whom thou gavest me, didst thou bid her to torment me with stripes, and the dungeon, and the dark, and solitude, and hunger? Nay, by Allhallows! he said, nor thought of it; trust me she shall pay therefor if so she hath done. She said: I crave no vengeance, but mercy I crave, and thou mayst give it me.

She tells him of the chaplain

She telleth of Dame Elinor

Then were they both silent, till he said: Now I, for my part, will pray thee bear what thou must bear, which shall be nought save this, that thy queenship lie quiet for a while; nought else of evil shall betide thee henceforth; but as much of pleasure and joy as may go with it. But tell me, there is a story of thy snatching a holiday these two days, and of a young man whom thou didst happen on. Tell me now, not as a maiden to her father or warder, but as a great lady might tell a great lord, what betid betwixt you two: for thou art not one on whom a young and doughty man may look unmoved. By Allhallows! but thou art a firebrand, my Lady! And he laughed therewith.

The Earl asketh of Christopher

Goldilind flushed red exceeding; but she answered steadily: Lord Earl, this is the very sooth, that I might not fail to see it, how he thought me worth looking on, but he treated me with all honour, as a brother might a sister. Tell me, said the Earl, what like was this man? Said she: He was young, but strong beyond measure; and full doughty: true it is that I saw him with mine eyes take and heave up one of our men in his hands, and cast him away as a man would a clod of earth.

Of Christopher's prowess

The Earl knit his brow: Yea, said he, and that story I have heard from the men-at-arms also. But what was the man like of aspect?

Of Christopher's aspects

She reddened: He was of a most goodly body, she said, fair-eyed, and of a face well carven; his speech kind and gentle. And yet more she reddened. Said the Earl: Didst thou hear what he was, this man? She said: I deem from his own words that he was but a simple forester.

Christopher a woodman

Yea, quoth the Earl, a simple forester? Nay, but a woodman, an outlaw, a waylayer; so say our men, that he fell on them with the cry: A-Tofts! A-Tofts! Hast thou never heard of Jack of the Tofts? Nay, never, said she. Said the Earl: He is the king of these good fellows; and a perilous host they be. Now I fear me, if he be proven to be one of these, there will be a gallows reared for him to-morrow, for as fair and as doughty as he may be.

The woodman pardoned

She turned all pale, and her lips quivered: then she rose up, and fell on her knees before the Earl, and cried out: O sir, a grace, a grace, I pray thee! Pardon this poor man who was so kind to me!

The Earl raised her up and smiled, and said: Nay, my Lady Queen, wouldst thou kneel to me? It is unmeet. And as for this woodman, it is for thee to pardon him, and not for me; and since, by good luck, he is not hanged yet, thy word hath saved his neck. She sat down in her chair again, but still looked white and scared. But the Earl spake again, and kindly:

Now to all these matters I shall give heed, my Lady; wherefore I will ask leave of thee, and be gone; and to-morrow I will see thee again, and lay some rede before thee. Meantime, be of good cheer, for thou shalt be made as much of as may be, and live in mickle joy if thou wilt. And if any so much as give thee a hard word, it shall be the worse for them.

Therewith he arose, and made obeisance to her, and departed. And she abode quiet, and looking straight before her, till the door shut, and then she put her hands to her face and fell a-weeping, and scarce knew what ailed her betwixt hope, and rest of body, and love, though that she called not by its right name.

The Earl leaveth her

CHAPTER XIX. EARL GEOFFREY SPEAKETH WITH CHRISTOPHER

The Earl's intent as to Chris-topher

The Earl comes to Chris-topher

Chris-topher speaketh

NOW it is to be said that the Earl had had much tidings told him of Christopher, and had no intent to put him to death, but rather meant to take him into the company of his guard, to serve him in all honour; and that which he said as to hanging him was but to try Goldilind; but having heard and seen of her such as we have told, he now thought it good to have a privy talk with this young man. So he bade a squire lead him to where Christopher was held in ward, and went much pondering.

So the squire brought him to the self-same Littlest Guard-room (in sooth a prison) where Goldilind had lain that other morn; and he gave the squire leave, and entered and shut the door behind him, so that he and Christopher were alone together. The young man was lying on his back on the pallet, with his hands behind his head, and his knees drawn up, murmuring some fag-end of an old song: but when he heard the door shut to he sat up, and, turning to the new-comer, said: Art thou tidings? If so, then tell me quickly which it is to be, the gallows or freedom? Friend, said

the Earl sternly, dost thou know who I am?
Nay, said Christopher; by thine attire thou
shouldst be some great man; but that is of
little matter to me, since thou wilt neither bid
slay me, or let me go, for a heedless word.

Quoth the Earl: I am the master of the land *The Earl*
of Meadham, so there is no need to tell thee *tells of*
that I have thy life or death in my hand. Now *himself*
thou wilt not deny that thou art of the company of Jack o' the Tofts? It is sooth, said
Christopher. Well, said the Earl, thou art
bold then to have come hither, for thou sayest
it that thou art a wolf's-head and forfeit of thy
life. Now, again, thou didst take the Lady of
Meadham home to thy house yesterday, and *Chris-*
wert with her alone a great while. Now *topher's*
according to thy dealings with her thou dost *challenge*
merit either the most evil of deaths, or else it
may be a reward: hah! what sayest thou?

Christopher leapt up, and said in a loud
voice: Lord King, whatsoever I may be, I am
not each man's dastard; when I saw that pearl
of all women, I loved her indeed, as who should
not, but it was even as I had loved the Mother
of God had she come down from the altar
picture at the Church of Middleham of the
Wood. And whoso saith otherwise, I give him
the lie back in his teeth, and will meet him
face to face if I may; and then, meseems, it
will go hard with him.

Spake the Earl laughing: I will be no champion against thee, for I hold my skin and my bones of too much price thereto. And, moreover, though meseemeth the Blessed Virgin would have a hot lover in thee were she to come down to earth anigh thy dwelling, yet trow I thy tale, that thou hast dealt with my Lady in honour. Therefore, lad, what sayest thou, wilt thou be a man of mine, and bear arms for me, and do my will? Spake Christopher: Lord, this is better than hanging. Why, so it is, lad, said the Earl, laughing again, and some would say better by a good deal. But hearken! if thou take it, thou must abide here in Greenharbour; a long while maybe; yea, even so long as my Lady dwelleth here. Christopher flushed and said: Lord, thou art kind and gracious, and I will take thy bidding. The Earl said: Well, so it shall be then; and presently thou shalt go out of this guard-room a free man. But abide a while.

Therewith he drew a stool to him and sat down, and spake not for a long while; and Christopher abode his pleasure; at last spake the Earl: One day, mayhappen, we may make a wedding for thee, and that no ill one. Christopher laughed: Lord, said he, what lady will wed me, a no man's son? Said the Earl: Not if the Lord of Meadham be thy friend? Well then, how if the Lady and Queen of Meadham

made thee the wedding? Said Christopher: I
were liefer to make mine own wedding, whenso
I need a woman in my bed: I will compel no
woman, nor ask others to compel her.

The Earl rose up, and fell to pacing the
prison to and fro; and at last he stood over
against Christopher, and said: Hearken, forester: I will foretell thy fortune; it is that thou
shalt become great by wedding. Christopher
held his peace; and the Earl spake again:
Now is the shortest word best. We deem thee
both goodly and doughty, and would wed thee
to a great lady, even that one to whom thou
hast shown kindness in the wilderness. Said
Christopher: It is the wont of great lords to
mock poor folk, therefore I must not show
anger against thee. I mock thee not, said the
Earl; I mean nought, but as my words say.
Nay then, said Christopher, thou biddest me an
evil deed, great Lord. What I said was that I
would compel no woman; and shall I compel
her, who is the wonder of the world and my
very own Lady? Hold thy peace, sir fool, said
the Earl; let me tell thee that she is as like to
compel thee as thou her. And as to her being
thy Lady, she shall be thy Lady and wife
indeed; but not here, for above all things will
she get her away from Greenharbour, and thou
shalt be her champion, to lead her about the
world like a knight errant.

The Earl offers a great wedding

More of the said wedding

*A wonder
to Chris-
topher*
Now was Christopher so troubled that he knew not what countenance to make, and scarce might he get a word out of his mouth a long while. At last he said: Lord, I see that I must needs do thy will if this be no trap which thou hast set for me. But over-wonderful is, that a great lady should be wedded to a gangrel churl. The Earl laughed: Many a ferly fares to the fair-eyed, quoth he; and also I will tell thee in thine ear that this Lady may not be so great as her name is great. Did she praise her

*Needs
must the
Lady go
from
Green-
harbour*
life-days to thee? Nay, said Christopher; I mind me well, she called herself the poor captive. She said but sooth, quoth the Earl; and her going away from Greenharbour is instead of her captivity; and I tell thee it is by that only I may make her joyous. And now one word: thou that criest out For the Tofts in battle art not altogether unfriended, meseemeth.

Christopher looked up proudly and fiercely: he said: Forsooth, Lord, my friends are good, though thou callest them wolf-heads and gallows-meat. Champion, said the Earl laughing,

*The Earl
would win
friends*
that may well be sooth; and there are a many ups and downs in the world. Bethink thee that the time may come when thou and thy friends may wend to my help, and may win the names of knight and baron and earl: such hap hath been aforetime. And now I crave of thee, when thou comest back to the Tofts, to

bid Jack fall upon other lands than Meadham when he rideth, because of the gift and wedding that I give thee now. So, lad, I deem that thou hast chosen thy part; but let not the tale thereof go out of thy mouth, or thou wilt gab away thy wedding. Lo, thou, I leave this door open behind me; and presently shall the smith come here to do away thine irons; and I shall send a squire to thee to lead thee to a fair chamber, and to bring thee goodly raiment, and do thou play amongst thy fellows as one of the best of them; and show them, if thou wilt, some such feats in peace as yesterday thou showedst them in battle. And to-morrow there will be new tidings. And therewith he departed.

The freeing of Christopher

No worse than his word he was, and anon came the smith and the squire; and he was brought to a chamber, and raiment of fine linen and silk and embroidery was brought to him: and when he was new clad he looked like a king's son, whereas aforetime he looked like a God of the Gentiles of old. All men praised his beauty and his courtesy, and after dinner was, and they had rested, they bade him play with them and show them his prowess, and he was nought loth thereto, and did what he might in running and leaping, and casting of the bar, and shooting in the bow. And in all these things he was so far before everyone, that they

Men make friends with him

marvelled at him, and said it was well indeed that he had not been slain yesterday. As to wrestling, therein he might do but little; for all forbore him after the first man had stood before him, a squire, well learned in war, and long and tough, and deemed a very stark man; him Christopher threw over his shoulder as though he had been a child of twelve years. So wore the day at Greenharbour in merrier wise for all good folk than for many a day had been the wont there.

CHAPTER XX. OF THE WEDDING OF CHRISTOPHER AND GOLDILIND

EARLY on the morrow came the Earl unto Goldilind, and she received him gladly, as one who had fashioned life anew for her. And when he had sat down by her, he spake and said: Lady, thou cravedst of me yesterday two things; the first was freedom from the captivity of Greenharbour; and the second, life and liberty for the varlet that cherished thee in the wild-wood the other day. Now thy first asking grieved me, for that thou hast been tyrannously done by; and thy second I wondered at; but since I have seen the young man, I wonder the less; for he is both so goodly, and so mighty of body, and of speech bold and free, yet gentle and of all courtesy, that he is meet to be knight or earl, yea, or very king. Now, therefore, in both these matters I will well to do thy pleasure, and in one way it may be; and thou mayst then go forth from Greenharbour as free as a bird, and thy varlet's life may be given unto him, and mickle honour therewith. Art thou, then, willing to do after my rede and my commandment, so that both these good things may betide thee?

Now comes the Earl to Goldilind again

He praises Christopher

He biddeth her wed Christopher

Right willing am I, she said, to be free and happy and to save the life of a fair youth and kind. Then, said he, there is one thing for thee to do: that this day thou wed this fair and kind youth, and let him lead thee forth from Greenharbour; and, belike, he will bring thee to no ill stead; for his friends are mightier than mayhappen thou deemest.

She is wroth

She turned as red as blood at his word; she knit her brows, and her eyes flashed as she answered: Is it seemly for a King's daughter to wed a nameless churl? And now I know thee, Lord Earl, what thou wouldst do; thou wouldst be King of Meadham, and put thy master's daughter to the road. And she was exceeding wroth. But he said, smiling somewhat: Was it then seemly for the King's daughter to kneel for this man's life, and to go near to swooning for joy when it was granted to her?

He giveth her choice

Yea, she said, for I love him with all my body and soul; and I would have had him love me par amours, and then should I have been his mistress and he my servant; but now shall he be my master and I his servant. And still was she very wroth.

Quoth the Earl: As to the matter of my being King of Meadham, that will I be, whatever befall, or die in the place else. So if thou wilt not do my rede, then must the varlet whom thou lovest die, and at Greenharbour must thou abide with Dame Elinor. There is no help for it.

She shrieked out at that word of his, and well nigh swooned, lying back in her chair: but presently fell a-weeping sorely. But the Earl said: Hearken, my Lady, I am not without warrant to do this. Tell me, hast thou ever seen any fairer or doughtier than this youngling? Never, said she. So say we all, he said. Now I shall tell thee (and I can bring witness to it) that in his last hour the King, thy father, when he gave thee into my keeping, spake also this: that I should wed thee to none save the fairest and doughtiest man that might be found: even so would I do now. What then sayest thou?

The Earl tells of the dead King's word

Again he puts the choice before her

She answered not, but still wept somewhat; then said the Earl: Lady, give me leave, and I shall send thy women to thee, and sit in the great hall for an hour, and if within that while thou send a woman of thine to say one word, Yes, unto me, then is all well. But if not, then do I depart from Greenharbour straightway, and take the youngling with me to hang him up on the first tree. Be wise, I pray thee.

And therewith he went his ways. But Goldilind, being left alone a little, rose up and paced the chamber to and fro, and her tears and sobbing ceased; and a great and strange joy grew up in her heart, mingled with the pain

Goldilind is troubled

of longing, so that she might rest in nowise. Even therewith the door opened, and her women entered, Aloyse first, and she called to her at once, and bade her to find Earl Geoffrey in the great hall, and say to him: Yes. So Aloyse went her ways, and Goldilind bade her other women to array her in the best and goodliest wise that they might. And the day was yet somewhat young. Now it must be said of Earl Geoffrey that, in spite of his hard word, he had it not in his heart either to slay Christopher or to leave Goldilind at Greenharbour to the mercy of Dame Elinor.

CHAPTER XXI. OF THE WEDDING OF THOSE TWAIN

NOW were folk gathered in the hall, and the Earl Geoffrey was standing on the dais by the high-seat, and beside him a worthy clerk, the Abbot of Meadhamstead, a monk of St. Benedict, and next to him the Burgreve of Greenharbour, and then a score of knights all in brave raiment, and squires withal, and sergeants; but down in the hall were the men-at-arms and serving-men, and a half hundred of folk of the country side, queans as well as carles, who had been gathered for the show and bidden in. No other women were there in the hall till Goldilind and her serving-women entered. She went straight up the hall, and took her place in the high-seat; and for all that her eyes seemed steady, she had noted Christopher standing by the shot-window just below the dais.

Folk in the hall

Now when she was set down, and there was silence in the hall, Earl Geoffrey came forth and said: Lords and knights, and ye good people, the Lady Goldilind, daughter of the Lord King Roland that last was, is now of age to wed; and be it known unto you, that the King, her father, bade me, in the last words by

The Earl speaks

him spoken, to wed her to none but the loveliest and strongest that might be, as witness I can bring hereto. Now such a man have I sought hereto in Meadhamstead and the much-peopled land of Meadham, and none have I come on, however worthy he were of deeds, or well-born of lineage, but that I doubted me if he were so fair or so doughty as might be found; but here in this half-desert corner of the land have I gotten a man than whom none is doughtier, as some of you have found to your cost. And tell me all you, where have ye seen any as fair as this man? And therewith he made a sign with his hand, and forth strode Christopher up on to the dais; and he was so clad, that his kirtle was of white samite, girt with a girdle of goldsmith's work, whereby hung a good sword of like fashion, and over his shoulders was a mantle of red cloth-of-gold, furred with ermine, and lined with green sendall; and on his golden curled locks sat a chaplet of pearls.

Then to the lords and all the people he seemed so fair and fearless and kind, that they gave a great shout of welcome; and Goldilind came forth from her chair, as fair as a June lily, and came to Christopher and reached out her hand to him, but he refrained him a moment, so that all they could see how sweet and lovely a hand it was, and then he took it, and drew

He shows Chris-topher

The folk are glad

her to him, and kissed her mouth before them all; and still he held her hand, till the Abbot of Meadhamstead aforetold came and stood by them and blessed them.

Then spake the Earl again: Lo ye, here hath been due betrothal of these twain, and ye may see how meet they be for each other in goodliness and kindness. Now there lacketh nought but they should be wedded straightway; and all is arrayed in the chapel; wherefore if this holy man will come with us and do on his mass-hackle, our joy shall be fulfilled; save that thereafter shall feast and merriment await all you in this hall, and we shall be there to welcome all comers in this house of Greenharbour, whereas this our gracious Lady has long abided so happily.

The Earl bids the wedding

Man looked on man here and there, and smiled a little as he spake, but none said aught, for there were none save the Earl's servants there, and a sort of poor wretches.

So therewithal they went their ways to the chapel, where was the wedding done as grandly as might be, considering they were in no grander place than Greenharbour. And when all was done, and folk began to flow away from the chapel, and Goldilind sat shamefaced but strangely happy in a great stall of the choir, the Earl called Christopher unto him, and said: My lad, I deem that some great fortune

Of the wedding

*Of the
Earl and
Chris-
topher*

shall betide thee since already thou hast begun
so luckily. But I beseech thee mar not thy
fortune by coming back with thy fair wife to
the land of Meadham; or else it may be thou
shalt cast thy life away, and that will bring her
sorrow, as I can see well. He spake this
grimly, though he smiled as he spake. But he
went on more gently: I will not send you
twain away empty-handed; when ye go out
a-gates into the wide world, ye shall find two
fair horses for your riding, well bedight, and

*Of the
Earl's
gift*

one with a woman's saddle; and, moreover, a
sumpter beast not very lightly burdened, for
on one side of him he beareth a chest wherein
is, first of all, the raiment of my Lady, and
beneath it some deal of silver and gold and
gems; but on the other side is victual and drink
for the way for you, and raiment for thee,
youngling. How sayst thou, is it well? It is
well, Lord, said Christopher; yet would I have
with me the raiment wherewith I came hither,
and my bow and my sax. Yea, and wherefore,

*of rai-
ment
meet
for the
woodland*

carle? said Earl Geoffrey. Said the youngling: We be going to ride the wild-wood, and
it might be better for safety's sake that I be so
clad as certain folk look to see men ride there.
But he reddened as he spake; and the Earl
said: By Allhallows! but it is not ill thought
of; and, belike, the same-like kind of attire
might be better to hide the queenship of the

Lady from the wood-folk than that which now she weareth? True is that, Lord, quoth Christopher.

The Earl bids fetch the old raiment

Yet, said the Earl, I will have you go forth from the Castle clad in your lordly weed, lest folk of mine say that I have stripped my Lady and cast her forth: don ye your poor raiment when in the wood ye be. Therewith he called to a squire, and bade him seek out that poor raiment of the new-wedded youngling, and bow withal and shafts good store, and do all on the sumpter; and, furthermore, he bade him tell one of my Lady's women to set on the sumpter some of Goldilind's old and used raiment. So the squire did the Earl's will, and both got Christopher's gear and also found Aloyse and gave her the Earl's word.

Of Aloyse

She smiled thereat, and went straightway and fetched the very same raiment, green gown and all, which she had brought to Goldilind in prison that other day, and in which Goldilind had fled from Greenharbour. And when she had done them in the chest above all the other gear, she stood yet beside the horses amidst of the varlets and squires who were gathered there to see the new-wedded folk depart.

Presently then came forth through the gate those two, hand in hand, and Earl Geoffrey with them. And he set Goldilind on her horse himself, and knelt before her to say farewell, and therewith was Christopher on his horse, and him the Earl saluted debonairly.

But just as they were about shaking their reins to depart, Aloyse fell down on her knees before the Earl, who said: What is toward, woman? A grace, my Lord, a grace, said she. Stand up on thy feet, said the Earl, and ye, my masters, draw out of earshot.

Even so did they; and the Earl bade her speak, and she said: Lord, my Lady is going away from Greenharbour, and anon thou wilt be going, and I shall be left with the sleek she-devil yonder that thou hast set over us, and here there will be hell for me without escape, now that my Lady is gone. Wherefore I pray thee take me with thee to Meadham-stead, even if it be to prison; for here I shall die the worst of deaths. Earl Geoffrey smiled on her sourly, and said: If it be as I understand, that thou hast lifted thine hand against my Lady, wert thou wending with me, thou shouldst go just so far as the first tree. Thou mayst deem thyself lucky if I leave thee behind here. Nor needest thou trouble thee concerning Dame Elinor; little more shalt thou hear of her henceforward.

But Goldilind spake and said: My Lord Earl, I would ask grace for this one; for what she did to me she did compelled, and not of her free will, and I forgive it her. And moreover, this last time she suffered in her body for the helping of me; so if thou mightest do her asking I were the better pleased.   It shall be as thou wilt, my Lady, said the Earl, and I will have her with me and keep her quiet in Mead-hamstead; but, by Allhallows! had it not been for thy word we would have had her whipped into the wild-wood, and hanged up on to a tree thereafter.

Goldilind prays grace for Aloyse

Then Aloyse knelt before Goldilind and kissed her feet, and wept, and drew back pale and trembling.   But Goldilind shook her rein once for all now, and her apple-grey horse went forth with her; Christopher came after, leading the sumpter beast, and forth they went, and passed over the open green about the Castle, and came on to the wood-land way whereby Goldilind had fled that other time.

They depart

CHAPTER XXII. OF THE WOODLAND BRIDE-CHAMBER

T HEY rode in silence a good way, and it was some three hours after noon, and the day as fair and bright as might be. Christopher held his peace for sweet shame that he was alone with a most fair maid, and she his own, and without defence against him. But she amidst of her silence turned, now red, and now somewhat pale, and now and again she looked somewhat askance on him, and he deemed her looks were no kinder than they should be.

At last she spake, yet not looking on him, and said: So, Forester, now is done what I must needs do: thy life is saved, and I am quit of Greenharbour, and its prison, and its torments: whither away then? Quoth he, all dismayed, for her voice was the voice of anger: I wot not whither, save to the house thou hast blessed already with thy dear body. At that word she turned quite pale, and trembled, and spake not for a while, and smote her horse and hastened on the way, and he after her; but when he was come up with her again, then she said, still not looking at him: A house of woodmen and wolf-heads. Is that a meet

They are on the road

Whither shall she go

dwelling-place for me? Didst thou hear men
at Greenharbour say that I am a Queen? Hear
them I did, quoth he; but meseemeth nought
like a Queen had they done with thee. She
said: And dost thou mock me with that? thou?
And she burst out weeping. He answered
not, for sore grief smote him, remembering her
hand in his but a little while ago. And again
she hurried on, and he followed her. *She weepeth*

When he came up with her she said: And
thou, didst thou woo me as a Queen? Lady,
he said, I wooed thee not at all; I was given
to thee, would I, would I not: great joy was
that to me. Then said she: Thou sayest
sooth, thou hast not wooed me, but taken me.
She laughed therewith, as one in bitterness. *Still she is wroth*
But presently she turned to him, and he won-
dered, for in her face was longing and kindness
nought like to her words. But he durst not
speak to her lest he should anger her, and she
turned her face from him again: and she said:
Wert thou given to me? meseems I was given
to thee, would I, would I not; the Queen to
the Churl, the Woodman, the Wolf-head. And
again she rode on, and he followed, sick at
heart and wondering sorely.

When they were riding together again, they
spake not to each other, though she stole
glances at him to see how he fared; but he
rode on with knit brows and a stern counte-

nance. So in a while she began to speak to him again, but as if there were nought but courtesy between them, and neither love nor hatred. She fell to asking him of wood-land matters, concerning bird and beast and things creeping; and at first he would scarce answer her at all, and then were his answers short; but at last, despite of all, he began to forget both grief and anger, so much the sweetness of her speech wound about his heart; and, withal, she fell to asking him of his fellows and their life in the woods, and of Jack of the Tofts and the like; and now he answered her

questions fully, and whiles she laughed at his words, and he laughed also; and all pleasure had there been of this converse, if he had not beheld her from time to time and longed for the fairness of her body, and feared her wrath at his longing.

So wore the day, and the sun was getting low, and they were come to another wood-land pool which was fed by a clear-running little brook, and up from it went a low bank of greensward exceeding sweet, and beyond that

oak trees wide-branched and great, and still fair greensward beneath them and hazel-thicket beyond them. There, then, Goldilind reined up, and looked about her, but Christopher looked on her and nought else. But she said: Let to-morrow bring counsel; but now am I weary to-night, and if we are not to ride night-long, we shall belike find no better place to rest in. Wilt thou keep watch while I sleep? Yea, he said, bowing his head to her soberly; and therewith he got off his horse, and would have helped her down from hers, but she slipped lightly down and stood before him face to face, and they were very nigh to each other, she standing close to her horse. Her face was pale to his deeming, and there was a piteous look in her eyes, so that he yearned towards her in his bowels, and reached his hands toward her; but she shrank aback, leaning against her horse, and said in a trembling voice, looking full at him, and growing yet paler: Forester, dost thou think it seemly that thou shouldst ride with us, thou such as thou hast told thyself to be, in this lordly raiment, which they gave thee yonder as part of the price for thy leading us away into the wild-wood?

Lady, said he, whether it be seemly or not, I see it is thy will that I should go clad as a wood-land churl; abide a little, and thy will shall be done. Therewith he did off the burden from the sumpter horse, and set the chests on the earth; then he took her horse gently, and led him with the other two in under the oak trees, and there he tethered them so that they could bite the grass; and came back thereafter, and took his old raiment out of the

She lighteth down

She would have him shift his raiment

chest, and said: What thou wilt have me do, I
will do now; and this all the more as to-morrow
I should have done it unbidden, and should
have prayed thee to do on garments less glorious than now thou bearest; so that we may
look the less strange in the wood-land if we
chance to fall in with any man.

Nought she answered as he turned toward
the hazel-copse; she had been following him
with her eyes while he was about that business,
and when his back was turned, she stood a
moment till her bosom fell a-heaving, and she
wept; then she turned her about to the chest
wherein was her raiment, and went hastily and
did off her glorious array, and did on the green
gown wherewith she had fled, and left her feet
bare withal.   Then she looked up and saw
Christopher, how he was coming from out the
hazel-thicket new clad in his old raiment, and
she cried out aloud, and ran toward him.   But
he doubted that some evil had betid, and that
she was chased; so he drew out his sword;
but she ran up to him and cried out: Put up
thy sword, here is none save me.

But he stood still, gazing on her in wonder-
ment, and now she was drawn near to him she
stood still before him, panting.   Then he said:
Nay, Lady, for this night there was no need of
thy disguising thee, to-morrow it had been
soon enough.   She said: I were fain if thou

wouldst take my hand, and lead me back to
our resting-place.

Even so he did, and as their palms met he
felt how her hand loved him, and a flood of
sweetness swept over his heart, and made an
end of all its soreness.   But he led her quietly
back again to their place.   Then she turned to
him and said: Now art thou the wood-land
god again, and the courtier no more; so now
will I worship thee.   And she knelt down
before him, and embraced his knees and kissed
them; but he drew her up to him, and cast his
arms about her, and kissed her face many
times; and said: Now art thou the poor captive again.   She said: Now hast thou forgiven
me; but I will tell thee that my wilfulness and
folly was not all utterly feigned; though when
I was about it, I longed for thee to break it
down with the fierceness of a man, and bid me
look to it how helpless I was, and thou how
strong and my only defence.   Not utterly
feigned it was: for I will say it, that I was
grieved to the heart when I bethought me of
Meadhamstead and the seat of my fathers.
What sayest thou then?   Shalt thou be ever a
woodman in these thickets, and a follower of
Jack of the Tofts?   If so thou wilt, it is well.

He took her by the shoulders and bent her
backwards to kiss her, and held her up above
the earth in his arms, waving her this way and

*She
kneeleth
to him*

*She
yieldeth
her*

that, till she felt how little and light she was in his grasp, though she was no puny woman; then he set her on her feet again, and laughed in her face, and said: Sweetling, let to-morrow bring counsel. But now let it all be: thou hast said it, thou art weary; so now will I dight thee a bed of our mantles, and thou shalt lie thee down, and I shall watch thee as thou badest me.

Therewith he went about, and plucked armfuls of the young bracken, and made a bed wide and soft, and spread the mantles thereover.

But she stood awhile looking on him; then she said: Dost thou think to punish me for my wilful folly, and to shame me by making me speak to thee? Nay, he said, it is not so. She said: I am not shamed in that I say to thee; if thou watch this night, I will watch by thee; and if I lie down to rest this night, thou shalt lie by me. For my foemen have given me to thee; and now shalt thou give thyself to me.

So he drew near to her shyly, like unto one who hath been forgiven. And there was their bridal bed, and nought but the oak boughs betwixt them and the bare heavens.

CHAPTER XXIII. THEY FALL IN WITH FRIENDS

NOW awoke Goldilind when the morning was young and fresh, and she drew the mantle up over her shoulders; and as she did so, but half awake, she deemed she heard other sounds than the singing of the blackbirds and throstles about the edge of the thicket, and she turned her eyes toward the oak trees and the hazel-thicket, and saw at once three of mankind coming on foot over the greensward toward her. She was afraid, so that she durst not put out a hand to awaken Christopher, but sat gazing on those three as they came toward her; she saw that two were tall men, clad much as Christopher; but presently she saw that there was a woman with them, and she took heart somewhat thereat; and she noted that one of the men was short-haired and dark-haired, and the other had long red hair falling about his shoulders; and as she put out her hand and laid it on Christopher's shoulder, the red-haired one looked toward her a moment under the sharp of his hand (for the sun was on their side), and then set off running, giving out a great whoop therewithal. Even therewith

Folk come in the morning

Two men and a woman

leapt up Christopher, still half awake, and the red-haired man ran right up to him, and caught him by the shoulders, and kissed him on both cheeks; so that Goldilind saw that these were the fellows whereof Christopher had told, and she stood there shamefast and smiling.

Presently came up the others, to wit, Gilbert and Joanna, and they also kissed and embraced Christopher, and all they were as full of joy as might be. Then came Joanna to Goldilind, and said: I wot not who this may be, brother, yet meseems she will be someone who is dear to thee, wherefore is she my sister. And therewith she kissed Goldilind; and she was kind, and sweet of flesh, and goodly of body, and Goldilind rejoiced in her. Joanna made much of her, and said to her: Here is to do, whereas two men have broken into a lady's chamber; come, sister, let us to the thicket, and I will be thy tiring-maid, and while these others tell their tales we shall tell ours. And she took her hand, and they went into the hazels; but the two new-come men seemed to find it hard to keep their eyes off Goldilind, till the hazels had hidden her.

Then turned David to Christopher, and said: Thy pardon, little King, that we have waked thee so early; but we wotted not that thou hadst been amongst the wood-women; and, sooth to say, my lad, we had little ease till we found thee, after we came home and saw all those hoof-marks yonder. Yea, said Gilbert, if we had lost thee we had been finely holpen up, for we could neither have gone back to the Tofts nor into the kingdom: for I think my father would have hanged us if we had come back with a By the way, Christopher is slain. But tell us, lad, what hath befallen thee with yonder sweetling. Yea, tell us, said David, and sit down here betwixt us, with thy back to the hazel-thicket, or we shall get no tale out of thee: tush, man, Joanna will bring her back; and that right soon, I hope.

Christopher laughed, and sat down between them, and told all how it had gone with him, and of Goldilind, who she was. The others hearkened heedfully, and Gilbert said: With all thou hast told us, brother, it is clear we shall find it hard to dwell in Littledale; so soon as thy loveling hath rested her at our house, we must go our ways to the Tofts and take counsel of our father.

Christopher yea-said this, and therewithal was come Joanna leading Goldilind duly arrayed (yet still in her green gown, for she would none other), fresh, blushing, and all lovely; and David and Christopher did obeisance before her as to a great lady; but she hailed them as brothers, merrily and kindly, and bade them kiss

The tale of the tidings

The women back again

her; and they kissed her cheek, but shyly, and especially David.

Thereafter they broke their fast under the oak trees, and spent a merry hour, and then departed, the two women riding the horses, the others afoot; so came they to the house of Littledale, some while before sunset, and were merry and glad there. Young they were, troubles were behind them, and many a joy before them.

CHAPTER XXIV. THEY TAKE COUNSEL AT LITTLEDALE

TEN days they abode in the house of
Littledale in all good cheer, and
Joanna led Goldilind here and there
about the woods, and made much of
her, so that the heart within her was full of joy,
for the freedom of the wild-woods and all the
life thereof was well-nigh new to her; whereas
on the day of her flight from Greenharbour,
and on two other such times, deadly fear, as is
aforesaid, was mingled with her joyance, and
would have drowned it utterly, but for the
wilfulness which hardened her heart against
the punishment to come. But now she was
indeed free, and it seemed to her, as to Christopher when he was but new healed of his
hurt, as if all this bright beauty of tree and
flower, and beast and bird, was but made for
her alone, and she wondered that her fellow
could be so calm and sedate amidst of all this
pleasure. And now, forsooth, was her queen-
hood forgotten, and better and better to her
seemed Christopher's valiant love; and the
meeting in the hall of the eventide was so
sweet to her, that she might do little but stand
trembling whiles Christopher came up to her,

*The joy
of the
woods*

*Happy is
Goldilind*

and Joanna's trim feet were speeding her over the floor to meet her man, that she might be a sharer in his deeds of the day.

Many tales withal Joanna told the Queen of the deeds of her husband and his kindred, and of the freeing of her and the other three from their captivity at Wailing Knowe, and of the evil days they wore there before the coming of their lads, which must have been worser by far, thought Goldilind, than the days of Greenharbour; so with all these tales, and the happy days in the house of the wild-woods, Goldilind now began to deem of this new life as if there had been none other fated for her, so much a part was she now become of the days of those woodmen and wolf-heads.

But when the last of those ten days was wearing to an end, and those five were sitting happy in the hall (albeit David sat somewhat pensive, now staring at Goldilind's beauty, now rising from his seat to pace the floor restlessly), Gilbert spake and said: Brethren, and thou, Queen Goldilind, it may be that the time is drawing near for other deeds than letting fly a few shafts at the dun deer, and eating our meat, and singing old songs as we lie at our ladies' feet; for though we be at peace here in the wild-wood, forgetting all things save those that are worthy to be remembered, yet in the cities and the courts of kings guile is not forgotten,

and pride is alive, and tyranny, and the sword *Gilbert's*
is whetted for innocent lives, and the feud is *words*
eked by the destruction of those who be sackless of its upheaving. Wherefore it behoveth
to defend us by the ready hand and the bold
heart and the wise head. So, I say, let us loiter
here no longer, but go our ways to-morrow to
the Tofts, and take the rede of our elders.
How say ye, brethren?

Quoth Christopher: Time was, brother, *He*
when what thou sayest would have been as a *biddeth*
riddle to me, and I would have said: Here are *fare to*
we merry, though we be few; and if ye lack *the Tofts*
more company, let me ride to the Tofts and
come back with a half score of lads and lasses,
and thus let us eke our mirth; and maybe they
will tell us whitherward to ride. But now
there is a change, since I have gained a gift *Chris-*
over-great for me, and I know that they shall *topher*
be some of the great ones who would be eager *yea-says*
to take it from me; and who knows what guile *it*
may be about the weaving even now, as on the
day when thou first sawest this hall, beloved.

Goldilind spake and sighed withal: Whither
my lord will lead me, thither will I go; but
here is it fair and sweet and peaceful; neither
do I look for it that men will come hither to
seek the Queen of Meadham.

David said: Bethink thee, though, my Lady,
that he who wedded thee to the woodman may

*Fear of
the foe*

yet rue, and come hither to undo his deed, by slaying the said woodman, and showing the Queen unto the folk.

Goldilind turned pale; but Joanna spake: Nay, brother David, why wilt thou prick her heart with this fear? For my part, I think that, chance-hap apart, we might dwell here for years in all safety, and happily enough maybe. Yet also I say that we of the Tofts may well

*They are
all at one
on this*

be eager to show this jewel to our kindred, and especially to our father and mother of the the Tofts; so to-morrow we will set about the business of carrying her thither, will she, nill she. And therewith she threw her arms about Goldilind, and clipped her and kissed her; and Goldilind reddened for pleasure and for joy that she was so sore prized by them all.

CHAPTER XXV. NOW THEY ALL COME TO THE TOFTS

NEXT morning, while the day was yet young, they rode together, all of them, the nighest way to the Tofts, for they knew the wood right well. Again they slept one night under the bare heavens, and, rising betimes on the morrow, came out under the Tofts some four hours after high noon, on as fair and calm a day of early summer as ever was seen.

They rode up straight to the door of the great hall, and found but few folk about, and those mostly women and children; Jack was ridden abroad, they said, but they looked to see him back to supper, him and his sons, for he was no great way gone.

Meantime, when they got off their horses, the women and children thronged round about them; and the children especially about Christopher, whom they loved much. The maidens, also, would not have him pass into the hall unkissed, though presently, after their faces had felt his lips, they fell a-staring and wondering at Goldilind, and when Christopher took her by the hand and gave her welcome to the House of the Tofts, and they saw that she was

They ride the wood-land

The children at the Tofts

They have good welcome

his, they grew to be somewhat afraid, or it might be shy, both of her and of him.

Anyhow, folk came up to them in the hall, and made much of them, and took them unto chambers and washed their feet, and crowned them with flowers, and brought them into the hall again, and up on to the dais, and gave them to eat and drink. Thither came to them also the Lady Margaret, Jack's wedded wife, and made them the most cheer that she might; and unto her did Christopher tell his story as unto his very mother; and what there was in the house, both of carle and of quean, gathered round about to hearken, and Christopher nothing loth. And Goldilind's heart warmed toward that folk, and in sooth they were a goodly people to look on, and frank and happy, and of all good will, and could well of courtesy, though it were not of the courts.

Goldilind loves that folk

Wore the bright day, and it drew toward sunset, and now the carles came straight into the hall by twos and threes, till there were a many within its walls. But to each one of these knots as they entered, someone, carle or quean, spake a word or two, and straightway the new-comers went up to the dais and greeted Christopher pleasantly, and made obeisance to Goldilind.

Come folk into the hall

At last was the hall, so quiet erst, grown busy as a beehive, and amidst the throng thereof came in the serving-folk, women and men, and set the endlong boards up (for the high table was a standing one of oak, right thick and strong); and then they fell to bringing in the service, all but what the fire was *Sunset* dealing with in the kitchen. And whiles this *without* was a-doing, the sun was sinking fast, and it was dusk in the hall by then it was done, though without the sky was fair and golden, and about the edges of the thicket were the nightingales singing loud and sweet, but within was the turmoil of many voices, whereof few heeded if their words were loud or soft.

Amidst all this, from close to the hall, rang *A horn* out the sound of many horns winding a wood- *and new-* land tune. None was afeard or astonied, *comers* because all knew it for the horns of Jack of the Tofts; but they stilled their chattering talk somewhat, and abided his coming; and even therewith came the sound of many feet and the clash of weapons, and men poured in, and there was the gleam of steel, as folk fell back to the right and left, and gave room to the new-comers. Then a loud, clear, and cheery voice cried out from amidst of them: Light in *Candle-* the hall, men and maids! Candles, candles! *rise* Let see who is here before us! *within*

Straightway then was there running hither and thither, and light sprang up over all the hall, and there could folk see Jack of the Tofts, and a score and a half of his best, every man of them armed with shield and helm and byrny, with green coats over their armour, and wreaths of young oak about their basnets; there they stood amidst of the hall, and every man with his naked sword in his fist. Jack stood before his folk clad in like wise with them, save that his head was bare but for an oak-wreath. Men looked on a while and said nought, while Jack looked proudly and keenly over the hall, and at last his eye caught Christopher's, but he made the youngling no semblance of greeting. Christopher's heart fell, and he misdoubted if something were not wrong; but he spake softly to one who stood by him, and said: Is aught amiss, Will Ashcroft? this is not the wont here. Said the other: Not in thy time; but for the last seven days it hath been the wont, and then off weapons and to supper peaceably.

CHAPTER XXVI.   OF THE KING OF OAKENREALM

EVEN therewith, and while the last word had but come to Christopher's ear, rang out the voice of Jack of the Tofts again, louder and clearer than before; and he said: Men in this hall, I bear you tidings! The King of Oakenrealm is amongst us to-night.

New tidings toward

Then, forsooth, was the noise and the turmoil, and cries and shouts and clatter, and fists raised in air and weapons caught down from the wall, and the glitter of spear-points and gleam of fallow blades. For the name of Rolf, King of Oakenrealm, was to those woodmen as the name of the Great Devil of Hell, so much was he their unfriend and their dastard. But Jack raised up his hand, and cried: Silence, ye! Blow up, horns, The Hunt's Up!

The Hunt up

Blared out the horns then, strong and fierce, under the hall-roof, and when they were done, there was more silence in the hall than in the summer night without; only the voice of the swords would not be utterly still, but yet tinkled and rang as hard came against hard here and there in the hush.

Again spake Jack: Let no man speak! Let

no man move from his place! I SEE THE KING!
Ye shall see him!

Therewith he strode up the hall and on to
the dais, and came up to where stood Christopher holding Goldilind's hand, and she all pale
and trembling; but Jack took him by the
shoulder, and turned him about toward a seat
which stood before the board, so that all men
in the hall could see it; then he set him down
in it, and took his sword from his girdle, and
knelt down before the young man, and took
his right hand, and said in a loud voice: I,
Jack of the Tofts, a free man and a sackless,
wrongfully beguilted, am the man of King
Christopher of Oakenrealm, to live and die for
him as need may be. Lo, Lord, my father's
blade! Wilt thou be good to me and gird me
therewith, as thy father girt him?

Now when Christopher heard him, at first he
deemed that all this was some sport or play
done for his pastime and the pleasure of the
hall-folk in all kindness and honour. But
when he looked in the eyes of him, and saw
him fierce and eager and true, he knew well it
was no jest; and as the shouts of men went up
from the hall and beat against the roof, himseemed that he remembered, as in a dream,
folk talking anigh him when he was too little
to understand, of a king and his son, and a
mighty man turned thief and betrayer. Then

his brow cleared, and his eyes shone bright, and he leaned forward to Jack and girt him with the sword, and kissed his mouth, and said: Thou art indeed my man and my thane and my earl, and I gird thee with thy sword as my father girded thy father.

Jack o' the Tofts taken to Earl

Then stood up Jack o' the Tofts and said: Men in this hall, happy is the hour, and happy are ye! This man is the King of Oakenrealm, and he yonder is but a thief of kings, a dastard!

And again great was the shouting, for carle and quean, young and old, they loved Christopher well: and Jack of the Tofts was not only their war-duke and alderman, but their wise man also, and none had any thought of gainsaying him. But he spake again and said: Is there here any old man, or not so old, who hath of past days seen our King that was, King Christopher to wit, who fell in battle on our behalf? If so there be, let him come up hither.

A greybeard witness

Then arose a greybeard from a bench nigh the high table, and came up on to the dais; a very tall man had he been, but was now somewhat bowed by age. He now knelt before Christopher, and took his hand, and said: I, William of Whittenham, a free man, a knight, sackless of the guilt which is laid on me, would be thy man, O my lord King, to serve thee in all wise; if so be that I may live to strike one stroke for my master's son, whom now I see,

A man taken to baron

the very living image of the King whom I served in my youth.

Then Christopher bent down to him and kissed him, and said: Thou art indeed my man and my thane and my baron; and who knows but that thou mayst have many a stroke to strike for me in the days that are nigh at hand.

Cometh an old carline

And again the people shouted: and then there came another and another, and ten more squires and knights and men of estate, who were now indeed woodmen and wolf-heads, but who, the worst of them, were sackless of aught save slaying an unfriend, or a friend's unfriend, in fair fight; and all these kneeled before him and put their hands in his, and gave themselves unto him.

The nurse of yore-agone

When this was done, there came thrusting through the throng of the hall a tall woman, old, yet comely as for her age; she went right up on to the dais, and came to where sat Christopher, and without more ado cast her arms about him and kissed him, and then she held him by the shoulders and cried out: O, have I found thee at last, my loveling, and my dear, and my nurse-chick? and thou grown so lovely and yet so big that I may never more hold thee aloft in mine arms, as once I was wont; though high enough belike thou shalt be lifted; and I say praise be to God and to his Hallows that thou art grown so beauteous and mighty a man!

Therewith she turned about toward the hall-throng and said: Thou, duke of these wood-men, and all ye in this hall, I have been brought hither by one of you; and though I have well-nigh died of joy because of the suddenness of this meeting, yet I thank him therefor. For who is this goodly and gracious young man save the King's son of Oakenrealm, Christopher that was; and that to my certain knowledge; for he is my fosterling and my milk-child, and I took him from the hands of the midwife in the high house of Oakenham a twenty-one years ago; and they took him from Oakenham, and me with him, to the house of Lord Richard the Lean, at Longholms, and there we dwelt; but in a little while they took him away from Longholms to I wot not whither, but would not suffer me to go along with him, and ever sithence have I been wan-dering about and hoping to see this lovely child again, and now I see him, what he is, and again I thank God and Allhallows therefor.

Once more then was there stir and glad tumult in the hall. But Goldilind stood won-dering, and fear entered into her soul; for she saw before her a time of turmoil and unpeace, and there seemed too much between her and the sweetness of her love. Withal it must be

She telleth of the sooth

Of Goldilind

She is
afraid

said, that for as little as she knew of courts and
war-hosts, she yet seemed to see lands without
that hall, and hosts marching, and mighty walls
glittering with spears, and the banners of a
great King displayed; and Jack of the Tofts
and his champions and good fellows seemed
but a frail defence against all that, when once
the hidden should be shown, and the scantiness
of the wood-land should cry on the abundance
of the kingdom to bow down.

They take
hands be-
fore the
folk

Now she came round the board and stood
beside Christopher, and he turned to her, and
stood up and took her hand, in such wise that
she felt the caress of it; and joy filled her
soul, as if she had been alone with him in the
wild-wood.

But he spake and said: All ye my friends;
I see and wot well that ye would have me sit
in my father's seat and be the King of Oakenrealm, and that ye will give me help and
furtherance therein to the utmost; nor will I
cast back the gift upon you; and I will say
this, that when I am King indeed, it is my
meaning and my will now, that then I shall be

Chris-
topher
speaketh

no less one of you good fellows and kind
friends than ye have known me hitherto; and
even so I deem that ye think of me. But, good
friends, it is not to be hidden, that the road ye
would have me wend with you is like to be
rough; and it may well be that we shall not

come to be kings or kings' friends, but men hunted, and often, maybe, men taken and slain. Therefore, till one thing or the other come, the kingship, or the taking, I will try to be no less joyous than now I am, and so meseemeth shall ye; and if ye be of this mind, then shall the coming days be no worse than the days which have been; and God wot they have been happy enough. Now again, ye see this most fair lady, whose hand I hold; she is my beloved and my wife; and therewithal she is the true Queen of Meadham, and a traitor sits in her place even as a traitor sits in mine. But I must tell you that when she took me for her beloved, she knew not, nor did I, that I was a King's son, but she took me as a woodman and outcast, and as a woodman and outcast I wooed her, trusting in the might that was in my body, and the love that was in my heart; and now before all you, my friends, I thank her and worship her that my body and my love was enough for her; as, God wot, the kingship of the whole earth should not be overmuch for her, if it lay open to her to take. But, sweet friends, here am I talking of myself as a King wedded unto a Queen, whereas meseemeth the chiefest gift our twin kingship hath brought you to-night is the gift of two most mighty unfriends for you; to wit, her foeman and mine. See ye to it, then, if the wild-wood

He telleth of his wife

And of his un-friends

yonder is not a meeter dwelling for us than this your goodly hall; and fear not to put us to the door as a pair of make-bates and a peril to this goodly company. Lo you, the sky without has not yet lost all memory of the sun, and in a little while it will be yellowing again to the dawn. Nought evil shall be the wild-wood for our summer dwelling; and what! ere the winter come, we may have won us another house where erst my fathers feasted. And thereto, my friends, do I bid you all.

But when they heard his friendly words, and saw the beauty of the fair woman whose hand he held, his face grew so well-beloved to them, that they cried out with so great a voice of cheer, wordless for their very joy, that the timbers of the Hall quavered because of it, and it went out into the wild-wood as though it had been the feastful roaring of the ancient gods of the forest.

But when the tumult sank a little, then cried out Jack of the Tofts: Bring now the mickle shield, and let us look upon our King.

So men went and fetched in a huge ancient shield, plated with berry-brown iron, inlaid with gold, and the four biggest men in the hall took it on their shoulders and knelt down anigh the dais, before Christopher, and Jack said aloud: King! King! stand up here! for this war-board of old days is the castle and the

He warneth the folk

The shield brought in

burg alone due to thee, and these four fellows
here are the due mountains to upbear it.

Then lightly strode Child Christopher on to
the shield, and when he stood firm thereon,
they rose heedfully underneath him till they
were standing upright on their feet, and the
King stood on the shield as if he were grown
there, and waved his naked sword to the four
orts.

*Chris-
topher
upraised
on shield*

Then cried out an old woman in a shrill
voice: Lo, how the hills rise up into tall mountains; even so shall arise Child Christopher to
the kingship.

*Child
Chris-
topher*

Thereat all folk laughed for joy and cried
out: Child Christopher! Child Christopher,
our King! And for that word, when he came
to the crown indeed, and ruled wide lands, was
he called Child Christopher; and that name
clave to him after he was dead, and but a name
in the tale of his kindred.

Now the King spake and said: Friends, now
is it time to get to the board, and the feast
which hath been stayed this while; and I pray
you let it be as merry as if there were no striv-
ing and unpeace betwixt us and the winning of
peace. But to-morrow we will hallow in the
Mote, and my earl and my barons and good
men shall give counsel, and then shall it be
that the hand shall do what the heart biddeth.

*They go
to table*

Therewith he leapt down from the shield,

and went about the hall talking to this one and that, till the board was full dight; then he took his place in the high-seat, beside Jack of the Tofts; and David and Gilbert and his other foster-brethren sat on either side of him, and their wives with them; and men fell to feasting in great glee.

But one thing there is yet to tell of this feast. When men had drunk a cup or two, and drunk memories to good men dead, and healths to good men living, amidst this arose a grey-head carle from the lower end of the hall, and said: *An old man* Child Christopher, thy grace, that I may crave a boon of thee on this day of leal service. Ask then, said Christopher, with a pleasant face. King, quoth the carle, here are all we gathered together, and we have before us the most beautifullest woman of the world, who sitteth by thy side; now to-night we be all dear friends, *He will have a boon* and there is no lack between us; yet who can say how often we may meet and things be so? I do not say that there shall enmity and dissension arise between us, though that may betide; but it is not unlike that another time thou, King, and thy mate, may be prouder than now ye be, since now ye are new to it. And if that distance grow between us, it will avail nought to ask my boon then. Well, well, ask it now, friend, said the King, laughing; I were fain of ending the day with a gift. This it is then,

King, said the carle: since we are here set
down before the loveliest woman in the world,
grant us this, that all we men-folk may for this
once kiss the face of her, if she will have it so.

 Huge laughter and cheers arose at his word;
but King Christopher arose and said: Friend,
thy boon is granted with a good will; or how
sayest thou, Goldilind my beloved? For all
answer she stood up blushing like a rose, and
held out her two hands to the men in the hall.
And straightway the old carle rose up and
went in haste to the high table, before another
man might stir, and took Goldilind by the chin,
and kissed her well-favouredly, and again men
laughed joyously. Then came before her Jack
of the Tofts and all his sons, one after other,
and kissed her face, save only David, who knelt
humbly before her, and took her right hand
and kissed it, while the tears were in his eyes.
Then came many of the men in the hall, and
some were bold, but many were shy, and when
they came before her durst kiss neither hand
nor face of her, but their hearts were full of
her when they went to their places again; and
all the assembly was praising her.

 So wore the time of that first night of the
kingship of Child Christopher.

*He would
men
should
kiss the
Queen*

*It is
granted*

*The end
of the
feast*

CHAPTER XXVII. OF THE HUSTING OF THE TOFTS

WHEN morning was, there were horns sounding from the tower on the toft, and all men hastening in their war-gear to the topmost of the other toft, the bare one, whereon was no building; for thereon was ever the mote-stead of these woodmen. But men came not only from the stead and houses of the Tofts, but also from the wood-land cots and dwellings anigh, of which were no few. And they that came there first found King Christopher sitting on the mound amidst the mote-stead, and Jack of the Tofts and his seven sons sitting by him,

and all they well-weaponed and with green coats over their hauberks; and they that came last found three hundreds of good men and true gathered there, albeit this was but the Husting of the Tofts.

So when there were no more to come, then was the Mote hallowed, and the talk began;

but short and sharp was their rede, for well did all men wot who had been in the hall the night before that there was now no time to lose. For though nigh all the men that had been in the hall were well known to each other, yet might there perchance have been some spy unknown, who had edged him in as a guest to one of the good men. Withal, as the saw saith: The word flieth, the wight dieth. And it were well if they might gather a little host ere their foeman might gather a mickle.

First therefore arose Jack of the Tofts, and began shortly to put forth the sooth, that there was come the son of King Christopher the old, and that now he was seeking to his kingdom, not for lust of power and gain, but that he might be the friend of good men and true, and uphold them and be by them upholden. And saith he: Look ye on the face of this man, and tell me where ye shall find a friend friendlier than he, and more single-hearted? And therewith he laid his hand on Christopher's head, and the young man rose up, blushing like a maid, and thereafter a long while could no lord be heard for the tumult of gladness and the clashing of weapons. *Jack telleth*

But when it was a little hushed, then spake Jack again: Now need no man say more to man on this matter, for ye call this curly-headed lad the King of Oakenrealm, even as some of ye did last night. *Christopher taken to King*

Mighty was the shout of yea-say that arose at that word; and when it was stilled, a greyhead stood up and said: King Christopher, and thou, our leader, whom we shall henceforth

*A tryst-
ing ap-
pointed*

call Earl, it is now meet that we shear up the war-arrow, and send it forth to whithersoever we deem our friends dwell, and that this be done at once here in this Mote, and that the hosting be after three nights' frist in the plain of Hazeldale, which all ye know is twelve miles nigher to Oakenrealm than this.

All men yeasaid this, no one gainsaid it; and straightway was fire kindled, and the bull slain, for the said elder had brought him thither; and the arrow was sheared and scorched and reddened, and the runners were fetched, and the word given them, and they were sped on their errand.

*A young
man
speaketh*

Uprose then another, a young man, and spake: Many stout fellows be here, and some wise and well-ruled, and many also hot-head and wilful: Child Christopher is King now, and we all know him, that when he cometh into the fray he is like to strike three strokes for two that any other winneth; but as to his lore of captainship, if he hath any, he was born with it, as is like enough, seeing who was his father; therefore we need a captain well-proven, to bid us how to turn hither and thither, and where to gather thickest, and where to spread thinnest; and when to fall on fiercely, and when to give way, and let the thicket cover us: for wise in war shall our foemen be. Now therefore if any one needeth a better captain than our kin-father and war-father Jack of the Tofts, he must needs go fetch him from otherwhere! How sayest thou, Christopher lad?

Jack is told of for Captain Christopher wills it

Great cheer there was at the word, and laughter no little therewith. But Christopher stood up, and took Jack by the hand, and said: Now say I, that if none else follow this man into battle, yet will I; and if none else obey him to go backward or forward to the right hand or to the left as he biddeth, yet will I. Thou, Wilfrid Wellhead, look to it that thou dost no less. But ye folk, what will ye herein?

So they all yea-said Jack of the Tofts for captain; and forsooth they might do no less, for he was wary and wise, and had done many deeds, and seen no little of warfare.

Then again arose a man of some forty winters, strong built and not ungoodly, but not merry of countenance, and he spake: King and war-leader, I have a word to say. We be wending to battle, we carles, with spear in fist and sword by side; and if we die in the fray, of the day's work is it; but what do we with our kinswomen, as mothers and daughters and wives and she-friends, and the little ones they have borne us? For, see ye! this warfare we are faring, maybe it shall not last long, and yet maybe it shall; and then may the foeman go about us and fall on this stead if we leave them behind here with none to guard them; and if,

Haward

on the other hand, we leave them men enough
for their warding, then we minish our host
overmuch.   What do we then?

Then spake Jack of the Tofts: This is well
thought of by Haward of Whiteacre, and we
must look to it.   And, by my rede, we shall
have our women and little ones with us; and
why not?   For we shall then but be moving
Toftstead as we move; and ever to some of us
hath it been as a camp rather than an house.
Moreover, ye know it, that our women be no
useless and soft queans, who durst not lie
under the oak boughs for a night or two, or
wade a water over their ankles, but valiant
they be, and kind, and helpful; and many of
them are there who can draw a bow with the
best, and, it maybe, push a spear if need were.
How say ye, lads?

Now this also they yea-said gladly; forsooth,
they had scarce been fain of leaving the women
behind, at least the younger ones, even had
they been safe at the Tofts; for there is no time
when a man would gladlier have a fair woman
in his arms than when battle and life-peril
are toward.

Thereafter the Mote sundered, when the
Captain had bidden his men this and that
matter that each should look to; and said that
he, for his part, with King Christopher and
a chosen band, would set off for Hazeldale

on the morrow morn, whereas some deal of the
gathering would of a certainty be come thither
by then; and that there was enough left of that
day to see to matters at the Tofts.

So all men went about their business, which
was, for the most part, seeing to the victualling
of the host.

*The
Husting
ended*

CHAPTER XXVIII. OF THE HOSTING IN HAZELDALE

Comes Goldilind and will fare with the men

ON the morrow early was Jack of the Tofts dight for departure, with Christopher and David and Gilbert and five score of his best men. But when they went out of the porch into the sweet morning, lo! there was Goldilind before them, clad in her green gown, and as fresh and dear as the early day itself. And Jack looked on her and said: And thou, my Lady and Queen, thou art dight as thou wouldst wend with us? Yea, she said, and why not? What sayest thou, King Christopher? said the Captain. Nay, said King Christopher, reddening, it is for thee to yea-say or nay-say; though true it is that I have bidden her farewell for two days' space. And the two stood looking on one another. But Jack laughed and said:

Jack yea-says it

Well, then, so be it; but let us get to the way, or else when the sweethearts of these lads know that we have a woman with us we shall have them all at our backs. Thereat all laughed who were within earshot, and were merry.

The road to Hazeldale

So they wended the wood-land ways, some afoot, some a-horseback, of whom was Jack of the Tofts, but Christopher and David went afoot. And Goldilind rode a fair white horse which the Captain had gotten her.

As they went, and King Christopher ever by Goldilind's right-hand, and were merry and joyous, they two were alone in the wood-land way; so Christopher took her hand and kissed it, and said: Sweetling, why didst thou tell me nought of thy will to come along with us? never had I balked thee. She looked at him, blushing as a rose, and said: Dear friend, I will tell thee; I knew that thou wouldst make our parting piteous-sweet this morning; and of that I would not be balked. See, then, how rich I am, since I have both parted from thee and have thee. And therewith she louted down from her saddle, and they kissed together sweetly, and so thereafter wore the way. *A reason given*

So came they to the plain of Hazeldale, which was a wide valley with a middling river winding about it, the wild-wood at its back toward the Tofts, and in front down-land nought wooded, save here and there a tree nigh a homestead or cot; for that way the land was builded for a space. Forsooth it was not easy for the folk thereabout to live quietly, but if they were friends in some wise to Jack of the Tofts. *Of Hazeldale*

So when the company of the Tofts came out into the dale about three hours after noon, it was no wonder to them to see men riding and going to and fro, and folk pitching tents and *Folk run to them* raising booths nigh to the cover of the wood; and when the coming of the Toft-folk was seen, and the winding of their horns heard, there was many a glad cry raised in answer, and many an horn blown, and all men there came running together toward where now was stayed Jack of the Tofts and Christopher and their men.

Talk of the King with the Queen

Then Goldilind bade Christopher help her light down; so he took her in his arms, and was not over hasty in setting her down again. But when she stood by him, she looked over the sunny field darkened by the folk hastening over the greensward, and her eyes glittered and her cheek flushed, and she said: Lord King, be these some others of thy men? Yea, sweetling, said he, to live and die with me. She looked on him, and said softly: Maybe it were an ill wish to wish that I were thou; yet if it might be for one hour! Said he: Shall it not be for more than one hour? Shall it not be for evermore, since we twain are become one? Nay, she said, this is but a word; I am but thine handmaid: and now I can scarce refrain my body from falling before thy feet. He laughed in her face for joy, and said: Abide a while, until these men have looked on thee, and then shalt thou see how thou wilt be a flame of war in their hearts that none shall withstand.

Now were the dale-dwellers all come together in their weapons, and they were glad of their King and his loveling; and stout men were they all, albeit some were old, and some scarce of man's age. So they were ranked and told over, and the tale of them was over six score who had obeyed the war-arrow, and more and more, they said, would come in every hour. But now the captains of them bade the Toft-folk eat with them; and they yea-said the bidding merrily, and word was given, and sacks and baskets brought forth, and barrels to boot, and all men sat down on the greensward, and high was the feast and much the merriment on the edge of Hazeldale.

Of the Dale-dwellers

They feast

CHAPTER XXIX. TIDINGS COME TO HAZELDALE

BUT they had not done their meat, and had scarce begun upon their drink, ere they saw three men come riding on the spur over the crown of the bent before them; these made no stay for aught, but rode straight through the ford of the river, as men who knew well where it was, and came on hastily toward the feasters by the wood-edge. Then would some have run to meet them, but Jack of the Tofts bade them abide till he had heard the tidings; whereas they needed not to run to their weapons, for, all of them, they were fully dight for war, save, it might be, the doing on of their sallets or basnets.

But Jack and Christopher alone went forward to meet those men; and the foremost of them cried out at once: I know thee, Jack of the Tofts! I know thee! Up and arm! up and arm! for the foemen are upon thee; so choose thee whether thou wilt fight or flee. Quoth Jack, laughing: I know thee also, Wat of White-end; and when thou hast told me how many and who be the foemen, we will look either to fighting or fleeing. Said Wat: Thou knowest the blazon of the banner which we saw, three red wolves running on a *Of the Lord Gandolf* silver field? Yea, forsooth, said Jack; 'tis the Baron of Brimside that beareth that shield ever; and the now Baron, hight the Lord Gandolf, how many was he? Said Wat: Ten hundreds or more. But what say ye, fellows? Quoth the other twain: More, more they were. Said Jack of the Tofts: And when shall he be here, deem ye? In less than an hour, said Wat, he will be on thee with great and small; but his riders, some of them, in lesser space.

Then turned Jack about and cried out for *David Sent to the Tofts for folk* David, and when he came, he said: Put thy long legs over a good horse, and ride straight back to the Tofts, and gather whatever may bear spear and draw bow, and hither with them, lad, by the nighest road; tarry not, speak no word, be gone!

So David turned, and was presently riding *They order their folk* swiftly back through the wood-land paths. But Jack spake to the bearers of tidings: Good fellows, go ye yonder and bid them give you a morsel and a cup; and tell all the tidings, and this, withal, that we have nought to flee from a good fightstead for Gandolf of Brimside. Therewith he turned to Christopher and said: Thy pardon, King, but these matters must be seen to straightway. Now do thou help me array our folk, for there is heart enough in them as in thee and me; and mayhappen we may make an end to this matter now and here. Moreover, the Baron of Brimside is a stout carle, so fight we must, meseemeth.

Then he called to them one of the captains of the Tofts, and they three spake together heedfully a little, and thereafter they fell to work arraying the folk; and King Christopher did his part therein deftly and swiftly, for quick of wit he was, and that the more whenso anything was to be done.

Of the array

As to the array, the main of the folk that were spearmen and billmen but moved forward somewhat from where they had dined to the hanging of the bent, so that their foemen would have the hill against them or ever they came on point and edge. But the bowmen, of whom were now some two hundreds, for many men had come in after the first tally, were spread abroad on the left hand of the spearmen toward the river, where the ground was somewhat broken, and bushed with thorn-bushes. And a bight of the water drew nearer to the Tofters, amidst of which was a flat eyot, edged with willows and covered with firm and sound greensward, and was some thirty yards endlong and twenty over-thwart. So there they abode the coming of the foe, and it was now hard on five o'clock.

Of the eyot in the river

But Christopher went up to Goldilind where she stood amidst of the spearmen, hand turning over hand, and her feet wandering to and fro almost without her will; and when he came to her, she had much ado to refrain her from falling on his bosom and weeping there. But he cried to her gaily: Now, my Lady and Queen, thou shalt see a fair play toward even sooner than we looked for; and thine eyes shall follow me, if the battle be thronged, by this token, that amongst all these good men and true I only wear a forgilded basnet with a crown about it. O! she said, if it were but over, and thou alive and free! I would pay for that, I deem, if I might, by a sojourn in Green-harbour again. What! he said, that I might have to thrust myself into the peril of snatching thee forth again? And he laughed merrily. Nay, said he, this play must needs begin before it endeth; and by Saint Nicholas, I deem that to-day it beginneth well. But she put her hands before her face, and her shoulders were shaken with sobs. Alas! sweetling, said he, that my joy should be thy sorrow! But, I pray thee, take not these stout-hearts for runaways. And Oh! look, look!

Christopher telleth Goldilind of the battle

She looked up, wondering and timorous, but all about her the men sprang up and shouted, and tossed up bill and sword, and the echo of their cries came back from the bowmen on the left, and Christopher's sword came rattling out of the scabbard and went gleaming up aloft.

Goldilind astonished

Then words came into the cry of the folk, and Goldilind heard it, that they cried Child Christopher! King Christopher! Then over her head came a sound of flapping and rending as the evening wind beat about the face of the wood; and she heard folk cry about her: The banner, the banner! Ho for the Wood-wife of Oakenrealm!

She seeth the foemen

Then her eyes cleared for what was aloof before her, and she saw a dark mass come spreading down over the bent on the other side of the river, and glittering points and broad gleams of white light amidst of it, and noise came from it; and she knew that here were come the foemen. But she thought to herself that they looked not so many after all; and she looked at the great and deft bodies of their folk, and their big-headed spears and

She is valiant

wide-bladed glaves and bills, and strove with her heart and refrained her fear, and thrust back the image which had arisen before her of Greenharbour come back again, and she lonely and naked in the Least Guard-chamber: and she stood firm, and waved her hand to greet the folk.

The folk hail her

And lo! there was Christopher kneeling before her and kissing her hand, and great shouts arising about her of The Lady of Oakenrealm! The Lady of Meadham! For the Lady! For the Lady!

CHAPTER XXX. OF THE FIELD THAT WAS SET IN THE HOLM OF HAZELDALE

NOW thither cometh Jack o' the Tofts, and spake to Christopher: See thou, lad; Lord King, I should say; this looketh not like very present battle, for they be stayed half way down the bent; and lo thou, some half score are coming forth from the throng with a white shield raised aloft. Do we in likewise, for they would talk with us. Shall we trust them, father? said Christopher. Trust them we may, son, said Jack; Gandolf is a violent man, and a lifter of other men's goods, but I deem not so evil of him as that he would bewray troth.

They will talk with the foemen

So then they let do a white cloth over a shield and hoist it on a long spear, and straightway they gat to horse, Jack of the Tofts, and Christopher, and Haward of White-acre, and Gilbert, and a half score all told; and they rode straight down to the ford, which was just below the tail of the eyot aforesaid, and as they went, they saw the going of the others, who were by now hard on the water-side; and said Jack: See now, King Christopher, he who rides first in a surcoat of his arms is even the

Jack telleth of the riding

Baron, the black bullet-headed one; and the next to him, the red-head, is his squire and man, Oliver Marson, a stout man, but fierce and grim-hearted. Lo thou, they are taking the water, but they are making for the eyot and not our shore; son mine, this will mean a hazeled field in the long run; but now they will look for us to come to them therein. Yea, now they are aland and have pitched their white shield. And hearken, that is their horn; blow we an answer: ho, noise! set thy lips to the brass.

So then, when one horn had done its song, the other took it up, and all men of both hosts knew well that the horns blew but for truce and parley.

Now come the Toft-folk to the ford, and take the water, which was very shallow on their side, and when they come up on to the eyot, they find the Baron and his folk off their horses, and lying on the green grass, so they also lighted down, and stood and hailed the new-comers. Then uprose the Lord Gandolf, and greeted the Toft-folk, and said: Jack of the Tofts, thou ridest many-manned to-day. Yea, Lord, said Jack, and thou also. What is thine errand? Nay, said the Baron, what is thine? As for mine host here, there came a bird to Brimside and did me to wit that I should be like to need a throng if I came thy

The others rear a white shield

They meet in the eyot

Jack talks with the Baron

way; and sooth was that. Come now, tell us what is toward, thou rank reiver, though I have an inkling thereof; for if this were a mere lifting, thou wouldst not sit still here amidst thy friends of Hazeldale.

Lord, said Jack o' the Tofts, thou shalt hear mine errand, and then give heed to what thou wilt do. Look to the bent under the wood, and tell me, dost thou see the blazon of the banner under which be my men? That can I not, said the Lord Gandolf; but I have seen the banner of Oakenrealm, which beareth the wood-woman with loins garlanded with oak-leaves, look much like to it at such a distance. *Of the banner*

Said Jack: It is not ill guessed. Yonder banner is the King's banner, and beareth on it the woman of Oakenrealm. The Lord bent his brows on him, and said: Forsooth, rank reiver, I wotted not that thou hadst King Rolf for thy guest.

Quoth Jack of the Tofts: Forsooth, Lord, no such guest as the Earl Marshal Rolf would I have alive in my poor house. Well, Jack, said the big Lord, grinning, arede me the riddle, and then we shall see what is to be done, as thou sayest. Lord, said Jack, dost thou see this young man standing by me? Yea, said the other, he is big enough that I may see him better than thy banner: if he but make old bones, as is scarce like, since he is of *Of the King* thy flock, he shall one day make a pretty man; he is a gay rider now. What else is he?

Quoth Jack of the Tofts: He is my King, and thy King, and the all-folk's King, and the King of Oakenrealm: and now, hearken mine errand: it is to make all folk name him King.

He of Brimside telleth his errand

Said the Lord: This minstrel's tale goes with the song which the bird sang to me this morning; and therefore am I here thronging; to win thy head, rank reiver, and this young man's head, since it may not better be, and let the others go free for this time. Hah! what sayest thou? and thou, youngling? 'Tis but the stroke of a sword, since thou hast fallen into my hands, and not in the hangman's or the King's.

Thou must win them first, Lord, said Jack of the Tofts. Therefore, what sayest thou? Where shall we cast down the white shield and uprear the red?

The Baron speaketh his mind

Hot art thou, head, heart, and hand, rank reiver, said the Lord; bide a while. So he sat silent a little; then he said: Thou seest, Jack of the Tofts, that now thou hast thrust the torch into the tow; if I go back to King Rolf without the heads of you twain, I am like to pay for it with mine own. Therefore hearken. If we buckle together in fight presently, it is most like that I shall come to my above, but thou art so wily and stout that it is not unlike that thou, and perchance this luckless youngling, may slip through my fingers into the wood; and then it will avail me little with the King that I have slain a few score nameless wolf-heads. So, look you! here is a fair field hazelled by God; let us two use it to-day, and fight to the death here; and then if thou win me, smite off my head, and let my men fight it out afterwards, as best they may without me, and 'tis like they will be beaten then. But if I win thee, then I win this youngling withal, and bear back both heads to my Lord King, after I have scattered thy wolf-heads and slain as many as I will; which shall surely befall, if thou be slain first.

He biddeth to holm gang

Then cried out Jack of the Tofts: Hail to thy word, stout-heart! this is well offered, and I take it, for myself and my Lord King here. And all that stood by and heard gave a glad sound with their voices, and their armour rattled and rang as man turned to man to praise their captains.

The joy of Jack

But now spake Christopher: Lord of Brimside, it is nought wondrous though thou set me aside as of no account, whereas thou deemest me no king or king's kindred; but thou, Lord Earl, who wert once Jack of the Tofts, I marvel at thee, that thou hast forgotten thy King so soon. Ye twain shall now wot that this is my

Speaks King Christopher

quarrel, and that none but I shall take this battle upon him.

He throws down his glove

Thou servant of Rolf, the traitor and murderer, hearken! I say that I am King of Oakenrealm, and the very son of King Christopher the old; and that will I maintain with my body against every gainsayer. Thou Lord of Brimside, wilt thou gainsay it? Then I say thou liest, and lo here, my glove! And he cast it down before the Lord.

Again was there good rumour, and that from either side of the bystanders; but Jack of the Tofts stood up silent and stiff, and the Baron of Brimside laughed, and said: Well, swain, if thou art weary of life, so let it be, as for me; but how sayest thou, Jack of the Tofts? Art thou content to give thine head away in this fashion, whereas thou wottest that I shall presently slay this king of thine?

The gibe of Jack

Said Jack: The King of Oakenrealm must rule me as well as others of his liege-men: he must fight if he will, and be slain if he will. Then suddenly he fell a-laughing, and beat his hand on his thigh till the armour rattled again, and then he cried out: Lord Gandolf, Lord Gandolf, have a care, I bid thee! Where wilt thou please to be buried, Lord?

Said the other: I wot not what thou wilt mean by thy fooling, rank reiver. But here I take up this youngling's glove; and on his head be his fate! Now as to this battle. My will is, that we two champions be all alone and afoot on the eyot. How say ye?

They talk of the battle

Even so be it, said Jack; but I say that half a score on each side shall be standing on their own bank to see the play, and the rest of the host come no nigher than now we are.

I yea-say it, said the Baron; and now do thou, rank reiver, go back to thy fellowship and tell them what we have areded, and do thou, Oliver Marson, do so much for our folk; and bid them wot this, that if any of them break the troth, he shall lose nought more than his life for that same.

Therewith all went ashore to either bank, save the Baron of Brimside and Christopher. And the Baron laid him down on the ground and fell to whistling the tune of a merry Yule dance; but as for Christopher, he looked on his foeman, and deemed he had seldom seen so big and stalwarth a man; and withal he was of ripe age, and had seen some forty winters. Then he also cast himself down on the grass, and fell into a kind of dream, as he watched a pair of wagtails that came chirping up from the sandy spit below the eyot; till suddenly great shouting broke out, first from his own bent, and then from the foemen's, and Christopher knew that the folk on either side had just heard of the battle that was to be on the holm.

The champions left alone

The hosts hear of the battle

The Baron arose at the sound and looked to
his own men, whence were now coming that
half-score who were to look on the battle from
the bank; but Christopher stirred not, but lay
quietly amongst the flowers of the grass, till he
heard the splash of horse-hoofs in the ford, and
there presently was come Jack of the Tofts
bearing basnet and shield for his lord. And
he got off his horse and spake to Christopher:
If I may not fight for thee, my son and King,
yet at least it is the right of thine Earl to
play the squire to thee: but a word before
thy basnet is over thine ears; the man yonder
is well-nigh a giant for stature and strength;
yet I think thou mayest deal with him, and be
none the sorer when thou liest down to-night.
To be short, this is it: when thou hast got a
stroke in upon him, and he falters, then give
him no time, but fly at him in thy wild-cat
manner and show what-like thews thou hast
under thy smooth skin; now thine helm lad.
So art thou dight; and something tells me
thou shalt do it off in victory.

CHAPTER XXXI. THE BATTLE ON THE HOLM

SO when Christopher was armed, Jack turned about speedily, and so gat him back through the ford and stood there on the bank with the nine other folk of the Tofts. And by this time was Gandolf of Brimside armed also, and Oliver Marson, who had done his helm on him, was gone to his side of the river.

Drew the huge man-at-arms then toward Christopher, but his sword was yet in the sheath: Christopher set his point to the earth and abode him; and the Baron spake: Lad, thou art fair and bold both, as I can see it, and Jack of the Tofts is so much an old foe of mine, that he is well-nigh a friend: so what sayest thou? If thou wilt yield thee straightway, I will have both thine head and the outlaw's with me to King Rolf, but yet on your shoulders and ye two alive. Haps will go as haps will; and it may be that ye shall both live for another battle, and grow wiser, and mayhappen abide in the wood with the reiver's men. Hah? What sayest thou?

Christopher laughed and said: Wouldest thou pardon one who is not yet doomed,

An offer of Gandolf

Baron?   And yet thy word is pleasant to us;
for we see that if we win thee, thou shalt be
good liege man of us.   Now, Baron, sword in
fist!

Gandolf drew his sword, muttering: Ah,
hah! he is lordly and kingly enough, yet may
this learn him a lesson.   Indeed the blade was
huge and brown and ancient, and sword and
man had looked a very terror save to one
great-hearted.

But Christopher said: What sayest thou
now, Baron, shall we cast down our shields to
earth?   For why should we chop into wood
and leather?   The Baron cast down his shield,
and said: Bold are thy words, lad; if thy deeds
go with them, it may be better for thee than
for me.   Now keep thee.

And therewith he leapt forward and swept
his huge sword around; but Christopher
swerved speedily and enough, so that the blade
touched him not, and the huge man had over-
reached himself, and ere he had his sword well
under sway again, Christopher had smitten
him so sharply on the shoulder that the mails
were sundered and the blood ran; and withal
the Baron staggered with the mere weight of
the stroke.   Then Christopher saw his time,
and leapt aloft and dealt such a stroke on the
side of his head, that the Baron tottered yet
more; but now was he taught by those two

terrible strokes, and he gathered all his heart to him and all the might of his thews, and leapt aback and mastered his sword, and came on fierce but wary, shouting out for Brimside and the King.

They fight wisely

Christopher cried never a cry, but swung his sword well within his sway, and the stroke came on Gandolf's fore-arm and brake the mails and wounded him, and then as the Baron rushed forward, the wary lad gat his blade under his foeman's nigh the hilts, and he gave it a wise twist and forth flew the ancient iron away from its master.

The last stroke

Gandolf seemed to heed not that he was swordless, but gave out a great roar and rushed at Christopher to close with him, and the well-knit lad gave back before him and turned from side to side, and kept the sword-point before Gandolf's eyes ever, till suddenly, as the Baron was running his fiercest, he made a mighty sweep at his right leg, since he had no more to fear his sword, and the edge fell so strong and true, that but for the byrny-hose he had smitten the limb asunder, and even as it was it made him a grievous wound, so that the Lord of Brimside fell clattering to the earth, and Christopher bestrode him and cried: How sayest thou, champion, is it enough? Yea, enough, and maybe more, said the Baron. Wilt thou smite off mine head? or what wilt

The fall of a champion

thou? Said Christopher: Here hath been enough smiting, meseemeth, save thy lads and ours have a mind to buckle to; and lo thou! men are running down from the bents towards us from both sides, yet not in any warlike manner

as yet. Now, Baron, here cometh thy grim squire that I heard called Oliver, and if thou wilt keep the troth, thou shalt bid him order thy men so that they fall not upon us till the battle be duly pitched. Then shalt thou be borne home, since thou canst not go, with no hindrance from us.

Now was Oliver come indeed, and the other nine with him, and on the other side was come Jack of the Tofts and four others.

*The
Baron
gives
himself
to Chris-
topher*

Then spake the Baron of Brimside: I may do better than thou biddest me; for now I verily trow herein, that thou art the son of Christopher the old; so valiant as thou art, and so sad a smiter, and withal that thou fearest not to let thy foeman live. So hearken all ye, and thou specially, Oliver Marson, my captain; I am now become the man of my lord King Christopher, and will follow him whereso he will; and I deem that will presently be to Oakenham, and the King's seat there. Now look to it that thou, Oliver, order my men under King Christopher's banner, till I be healed; and then if all be not over, I shall come forth myself, shield on neck and spear in fist, to do battle for my liege lord; so help me God and St. James of the Water!

Therewith speech failed him and his wit therewith; so betwixt them they unarmed him and did him what leechdom they might do there and then; and he was nowise hurt deadly: as for Child Christopher, he had no scratch of steel on him. And Oliver knelt before him when he had dight his own lord, and swore fealty to him then and there; and so departed, to order the folk of Brimside and tell them the tidings, and swear them liege men of King Christopher.

They swear allegiance

CHAPTER XXXII. OF GOLDILIND AND CHRISTOPHER

NOW Jack of the Tofts said a word to one of his men, and he rode straightway up into the field under the wood, and spake to three of the captains of the folk, and they ranked a hundred of the men, of those who were best dight, and upraised amongst them the banner of Oakenrealm, and led all them down to the river bank; and with these must needs go Goldilind; and when they came down thither, Christopher and Jack were there on the bank to hail them, and they raised a great shout when they saw their King and their Earl standing there, and the shout was given back from the wood-side; and then the men of Brimside took it up, for they had heard the bidding of their Lord, and he was now in a pavilion which they had raised for him on the mead, and the leeches were looking to his hurts; and they feared him, but rather loved than hated him, and he was more to them than the King in Oakenham, and they were all ready to do his will.

But as to Goldilind, her mind it had been, as she was going down the meadow, that she would throw herself upon Christopher's bosom and love him with glad tears of love; but as she came and stood over against him, she was abashed, and stood still looking on him, and spake no word; and he also was ashamed before all that folk to say the words whereof his heart was full, and longed for the night, that they might be alone together.

But at last he said: Lady and Queen, thou seest that we be well-beloved that they rejoice so much in a little deed of mine. And still she spake nought, and held hand in hand.

But Jack of the Tofts spake and said: By *Jack* St. Hubert! the deed may be little, though *praises* there be men who would think no little of *the battle* overcoming the biggest man and the fellest fighter of Oakenrealm, but at least great things shall come thereof. King, thy strokes of this day have won thee Oakenrealm, or no man I know in field; and many a mother's son have they saved from death. For look thou yonder over the river, Goldilind, my Lady, and tell me what thou seest. She turned to him and said: Lord Earl, I see warriors a many. Yea, said Jack, and stout fellows be they for the more part; and hard had been the hand-play had we met, ere they had turned their backs; but now, see thou, we shall wend side by side toward *His hope* Oakenrealm, for our Lord there hath won them *is high* to his friends; and doubt thou not that when they see him and thee anigh, they shall be

friends in deed.   What! dost thou weep for
this?   Or is it because he hath done the deed
and not thou? or rather, because thine heart is
full for the love of him?   She smiled kindly
on Jack, but even therewith she felt two hands
laid on her shoulders, and Christopher kissed
her without any word.

CHAPTER XXXIII. A COUNCIL OF CAPTAINS: THE HOST COMES TO BROADLEES, AND MAKES FOR WOODWALL

THAT night, though there was some little coming and going between the Tofters and the Brimsiders, yet either flock slept on their own side of the river. Moreover, before the midst of the night, cometh David to the wood-side, and had with him all men defensible of the Tofts and the houses thereabout, and most of the women also, many of whom bore spear or bow, so that now by the wood-side, what with them of the Tofts and the folk who joined them thereto from the country-side about Hazeldale, there were well-nigh ten hundreds of folk under weapons; and yet more came in the night through; for the tidings of the allegiance of Brimside was spreading full fast.

David brings folk to the host

Betimes on the morrow was King Christopher afoot, and he and Jack and David and Gilbert, and they twelve in company, went down to the banner by the water-side; and to them presently came Oliver Marson and ten other of the captains of Brimside, and did them to wit that the Baron were fain if they would

The Tofter Captains cross the water

come to his pavilion and hold counsel therein, for that he was not so sick but he might well speak his mind from where he lay. So thither they went all, with good will, and the Baron greeted them friendly, and made what reverence he might to Christopher, and bade him say what was his mind and his will. But Christopher bade them who were his elders in battle to speak; and the Baron laughed outright, and

The mind of the Baron

said: Meseemeth, Lord King, thou didst grow old yesterday at my costs; but since thou wilt have me to speak, I will even do so. And to make matters the shorter, I will say that I wot well what ye have to do; and that is, to fall upon the Earl Marshal's folk ere they fall upon us. Now some folk deem we should fare to Brimside and have a hosting there; but I say nay; whereas it lieth out of the road to Oakenham, and thereby is our road meseemeth; and it is but some six days' riding hence, save, as is most like, two of those days be days of battle. But if we go straight forward with

He would wend straight to Oakenham

banners displayed, each day's faring shall be a day of hosting and gathering; for I tell thee, Lord King, the fame of thee has by now gone far in this country-side. Wherefore I say no more, since I wax weary, than this: to the road this morning, and get we so far, as Broadlees ere night-fall, for there we shall get both victual and folk.

There was good cheer made at his word, so
Christopher spake: Baron of Brimside, thou
hast spoken my very mind and will; and but
if these lords and captains gainsay it, let us
tarry no longer, but array all our folk in good
order and take tale of them, and so for Broadlees.   What say ye, lords?

*They are
at one*

None nay-said it, so there was no more talk
save as to the ordering of this or the other
company. And it was so areded that the
Brimside men should fare first at the head of
the host with the banner of Brimside, and that
then should go the mingled folk of the
country-side, and lastly the folk of the Tofts
with the banner of Oakenrealm; so that if the
host came upon foemen, they might be for
a cloud to hide the intent of their battles
awhile till they might take their advantage.

*The
host ar-
rayed for
Broad-
lees*

So went the captains to their companies,
and the Tofters and their mates crossed the
river to the men of Brimside, who gave them
good cheer when they came amongst them;
and it was hard to order the host for a while,
so did the upland folk throng about the King
and the Queen; and happy were they who had
a full look on Goldilind; and yet were some so
lucky and so bold that they kissed a hand of
her; and one there was, a very tall young man,
and a goodly, who stood there and craved to
kiss her cheek, and she did not gainsay him,

*A bold
swain*

and thereafter nought was good to him save an occasion to die for her.

A good King

As for Christopher, he spake to many, and said to them that wheresoever his banner was, he at least should be at the fore-front whenso they came upon unpeace; and so soon as they gat to the road, he went from company to company, speaking to many, and that so sweetly and friendly that all praised him, and said that here forsooth was a king who was all good and nothing bad, whereas hitherto men had deemed them lucky indeed if their king were half good and half bad.

Broad-lees nought against them

Merry then was the road to Broadlees, and they came there before night-fall; and it was a little cheaping town and unwalled, and if the folk had had any will to ward them, they lacked might. But when they found they were not to be robbed, and that it was but the proclaiming of King Christopher in the market-place and finding victual and house-room for the host, and the Mayor taking a paper in payment thereof, none stirred against them, and a many joined the host to fight for the fair young King. Now nought as yet had they heard at Broadlees of any force stirring against them.

Tidings of war

But in the morning when they went on their ways again, and were bound for Cheaping Woodwall, which was a fenced town, they sent out well-horsed riders to espy the road, who came back on the spur two hours after noon, and did them to wit that there was a host abiding them beneath the walls of Woodwall under the banner of Walter the White, an old warrior and fell fighter; but what comfort he might have from them of Woodwall they wotted not; but they said that the tidings of their coming had gone abroad, and many folk were abiding the issue of this battle ere they joined them to either host. Now on these tidings the captains were of one mind, to wit, to fare on softly till they came to a defensible place not far from the foemen, since they could scarce come to Woodwall in good order before night-fall, and if they were unfoughten before, to push forward to battle in the morning.

Even so did they, and made halt at sunset on a pleasant hill above a river some three miles from Woodwall, and there they passed the night unmeddled with.

They make stay

CHAPTER XXXIV. BATTLE BEFORE WOODWALL

W HEN morning was, the captains came to King Christopher to council: but while they were amidst of their talk came the word that the foe was anigh, and come close to the river-bank; whereat was none abashed; but to all it seemed wisdom to abide them on the vantage-ground. So then there was girding of swords and doing on of helms; **as** for ordering of the folk, it was already done, for all the host was ranked on the bent-side, with the banner of Oakenrealm in the midst; on its left hand the banner of the Tofts, and on the right the banner of Brimside.

Now when Christopher was come to his place, he looked down and saw how the foemen were pouring over the river, for it was nowhere deep, and there were four quite shallow fords: many more were they than his folk, but he deemed they fared somewhat tumultuously; and when the bowmen of the Tofts began shooting, the foemen, a many of them, stayed amidst of the river to bend bow in their turn, and seemed to think that were nigh enough already; nay, some went back again to the other bank, to shoot thence the surer and the drier, and some went yet a little further back on the field. So that when their sergeants and riders were come on to the hither bank, they lacked about a fifth of all their host; and they themselves, for all they were so many, had some ado to make up their minds to go forward.

Evil order of the foemen

Forsooth, when they looked up to the bent and saw the three banners of Oakenrealm and the Tofts and Brimside all waving over the same ranks, they knew not what to make of it. And Christopher's host, when they saw them hang back, brake out into mocking whoops and shouts, and words were heard in them: Come and dine at Brimside, good fellows! Come up to the Tofts for supper and bed! A Christopher! A Christopher! and so forth. Now all King Christopher's men were afoot, saving a band of the riders of Brimside, who bestrode strong and tall horses, and bore jack and sallet and spear, but no heavy armour.

They taunt the foe

So Christopher heard and saw, and the heart rose high in him, and he sent messengers to the right and the left, and bade the captains watch till he waved his sword aloft, and then all down the bent together; and he bade the Brimside riders edge a little outward and downward, and be ready for the chase, and suffer not any of the foemen to gather together when once they fell to running; for he knew

Christopher will give token

in his heart that the folk before him would never abide their onfall. And the day was yet young, and it lacked four hours of noon.

Now they fall on

King Christopher abode till he saw the foemen were come off the level ground, and were mounting the bent slowly, and not in very good order or in ranks closely serried. Then he strode forth three paces, and waved his sword high above his head, and cried out: A Christopher! A Christopher! Forward, banner of the Realm! And forth he went, steady and strong, and a great shout arose behind him, and none shrank or lagged, but spears and bills, and axes and swords, all came on like a wall of steel, so that to the foemen the earth seemed alive with death, and they made no show of abiding the onset, but all turned and ran, save Walter the White and a score of his

The foemen run

knights, who forsooth were borne down in a trice, and were taken to mercy, those of them who were not slain at the first crash of weapons.

Of the over-throw

There then ye might have seen great clumps of men making no defence, but casting down their weapons and crying mercy; and forsooth so great was the throng, that no great many were slain: but on the other hand, but few gat away across the water, and on them presently fell the Brimside riders, and hewed down and slew and took few to mercy. And some few besides the first laggards of the bowmen, it might be three hundreds in all, escaped, and gat to Woodwall, but when they of the town saw them, they made up their minds speedily, and shut their gates, and the poor fleers found but the points of shafts and the heads of quarrels before them.

But on the field of deed those captives were somewhat fearful as to what should be done with them, and they spake one to the other about it, that they would be willing to serve the new King, since he was so mighty. And amidst of their talk came the captains of King Christopher, and they drew into a ring around them, and the lords bade them look to it whether they would be the foemen of the King, the son of that King Christopher the Old. If so ye be, said they, ye may escape this time; but ye see how valiant a man he is, and how lucky withal, and happy shall they be whom he calleth friends. Now what say ye, will ye take up your weapons again, and be under the best of kings and a true one, or will ye depart and take the chance of his wrath in the coming days? We say, how many of you will serve King Christopher?

Then arose from them a mighty shout: All! All! One and All! Albeit some there were who slunk away and said nought; and none heeded them.

So then all the sergeants and the common

Peace for the captives

They turn to Christopher's part

folk swore allegiance to King Christopher;
but of the knights who were left alive, some
said Yea, and some Nay; and these last
were suffered to depart, but must needs ride
unarmed.

*Of the
Wood-
wall folk*

Now by the time all was done, and the new
men had dined along with the rest of the host,
and of the new-comers tale had been taken, the
day was wearing; so they set off for Woodwall,
and on the way they met the Mayor and Aldermen thereof, who came before King Christopher
and knelt to him, and gave him the keys of
their town; so he was gracious to them, and
thanked them, and bade see to the victual and
lodging of the host, and that all should be paid
thereafter. And they said that they had seen

*They
make
peace*

to all this before they came forth of the town,
and that if the Lord King would ride forth, he
would find fair lodging in the good town. So
King Christopher was pleased, and bade the
burgesses ride beside him, and he talked merrily with them on the way, so that their hearts
rejoiced over the kindness of their lord.

*The King
and the
Queen
ride
Wood-
wall to-
gether*

So they came to the gate, and there the King
made stay till Goldilind was fetched to him, so
that they might ride into the good town side
by side. And in the street was much people
thronging, and the sun was scarce set, so that
the folk could see their King and Queen
what they were; and they who were nighest

unto them, they let their shouts die out, so were their hearts touched with the sight of them and the love of their beauty.

Thus rode they in triumph through the street till they were come to their lodging, which was great and goodly as for a cheaping town; and so the day was gone and the night was come, and the council and the banquet were over; then were the King and Goldilind together again, like any up-country lad and lass. But she stood before him and said: O thou King and mighty warrior, surely I ought to fear thee now, but it is not so, so sore as I desire thee; but yet it maketh both laughter and tears come to me when I think of the day when we rode away from Greenharbour with thee, and I seemed to myself a great lady, though I were unhappy; and though I loved thy body, I feared lest the churl's blood in thee might shame me perchance, and I was proud and unkind to thee, and I hurt thee sorely; and now I will say it, and confess, that somewhat I joyed to see thine anguish, for I knew that it meant thy love for me and thy desire to me. Lo now, wilt thou forgive me this, or wilt thou punish me, O Lord King?

He laughed. Sweetling, he said, meseemeth now all day long I have been fighting against raiment rather than men; no man withstood me in the battle, for that they feared the crown

Of Christo-pher and Goldilind

She asketh pardon

Chris-topher is kind

on my helm and the banner over my head; and when those good men of the town brought me the keys, how should I have known them from borrel folk but for their scarlet gowns and fur hoods? And meseemed that when they knelt to me, it was the scarlet gowns kneeling to the kingly armour. Wherefore, sweet-heart, if thou fearest that the King should punish thee for so wounding the poor Christopher of those few days ago, as belike thou deservest it, bid the King do off his raiment, and do thou in likewise, and then there shall be no King to punish, and no king's scather to thole the punishment, but only Christopher and Goldilind, even as they met erewhile on the dewy grass of Littledale.

They love together

She blushed blood-red; but ere his words were done, her hands · were busy with girdle and clasp, and her raiment fell from her to the earth, and his kingly raiment was cast from him, and he took her by the hand and led her to the bed of honour, that their love might have increase that night also.

CHAPTER XXXV.   AN   OLD
ACQUAINTANCE   AND   AN   EVIL
DEED

WHEN morning was, and it was yet *The host*
early, the town was all astir and *gathers*
the gates were thrown open, and *for de-*
weaponed men flocked into it *parture*
crying out for Christopher the King. Then
the King came forth, and Jack o' the Tofts
and his sons, and Oliver Marson, and the
captains of Brimside; and the host was blown
together to the market-place, and there was a
new tale of them taken, and they were now
hard on seventy hundreds of men. So then
were new captains appointed, and thereafter
they tarried not save to eat a morsel, but went
out a-gates, faring after the banners to Oakenrealm, all folk blessing them as they went.

Nought befell them of evil that day, but ever *They*
fresh companies joined them on the road; and *grow*
they gat harbour in another walled town, hight *greater*
Sevenham, and rested there in peace that
night, and were now grown to eighty hundreds.

Again on the morrow they were on the road
betimes, and again much folk joined them, and
they heard no tidings of any foeman faring
against them; whereat Jack o' the Tofts

marvelled, for he and others had deemed that
now at last would Rolf the traitor come out
against them. Forsooth, when they had gone
all day and night was at hand, it seemed most
like to the captains that he would fall upon
them that night, whereas they were now in a
somewhat perilous pass; for they must needs
rest at a little thorp amidst of great and thick
woods, which lay all round about the frank of
Oakenham, as a garland about a head. So
there they kept watch and ward more heedfully than their wont was; and King Christopher lodged with Goldilind at the house of a
goodman of the thorp.

Now when it lacked but half an hour of
midnight, and Jack o' the Tofts and Oliver
Marson and the Captain of Woodwall had just
left him, after they had settled the order of the
next day's journey, and Goldilind lay abed in
the inner chamber, there entered one of the
men of the watch and said: Lord King, here
is a man hereby who would see thee; he is
weaponed, and he saith that he hath a gift for
thee: what shall we do with him? Said Christopher: Bring him in hither, good fellow.
And the man went back, and came in again leading a tall man, armed, but with a hood done over
his steel hat, so that his face was hidden, and
he had a bag in his hand with something
therein.

Then spake the King and said: Thou man, *A gift*
since thy face is hidden, this trusty man-at-
arms shall stand by thee while we talk together.
Lord, said the man, let there be a dozen to
hear our talk I care not; for I tell thee that I
come to give thee a gift, and gift-bearers are
oftenest welcome. Quoth the King: Maybe,
yet before thou bring it forth I would see thy
face, for meseems I have an inkling of thy
voice.

So the man cast aback his hood, and lo, it *Simon*
was Simon the squire. Hah! said Christo- *is there*
pher, it is thou then! hast thou another knife
to give me? Nay, said Simon, only the work of
the knife. And therewith he set his hand to
the bag and drew out by the hair a man's
head, newly hacked off and bleeding, and said:
Hast thou seen him before, Lord? He was a
great man yesterday, though not so great as
thou shalt be to-morrow.

Once only I have seen him, said Christo- *Simon*
pher, and then he gave me this gift (and he *speaketh*
showed his father's ring on his finger); thou *for him-*
hast slain the Earl Marshal, who called himself *self*
the King of Oakenrealm: my traitor and
dastard, he was but thy friend. Wherefore
have I two evil deeds to reward thee, Simon,
the wounding of me and the slaying of him.
Dost thou not deem thee gallows-ripe? King,
said Simon, what wouldst thou have done with

him hadst thou caught him? Said Christopher: I had slain him had I met him with a weapon in his fist; and if we had taken him I had let the folk judge him. Said Simon: That is to say, that either thou hadst slain him thyself, or bidden others to slay him. Now then I ask thee, King, for which deed wilt thou slay me, for not slaying thee, or for doing thy work and slaying thy foe?

Said Christopher to the guard: Good fellow, fetch here a good horse ready saddled and bridled, and be speedy.

Christopher bids Simon depart

So the man went; and Christopher said to Simon: For the knife in my side, I forgive it thee; and as to the slaying of thy friend, it is not for me to take up the feud. But this is no place for thee: if Jack of the Tofts, or any of his sons, or one of the captains findeth thee, soon art thou sped; wherefore I rede thee, when yonder lad hath brought thee the horse, show me the breadth of thy back, and mount the beast, and put the most miles thou canst betwixt me and my folk; for they love me.

Payment for the felon

Said Simon: Sorry payment for making thee a King! Said Christopher: Well, thou art in the right; I may well give gold for getting rid of such as thou. And he put his hand into a pouch that hung on his chair, and drew out thence a purse, and gave it unto Simon, who took it and opened it and looked therein, and

A felon's deed once more and the reward thereof

then flung it down on the ground. Christopher looked on him wrathfully with reddened face, and cried out: Thou dog! wouldst thou be an earl and rule the folk? What more dost thou want? This! cried out Simon, and leapt upon him, knife aloft. Christopher was unarmed utterly; but he caught hold of the felon's right arm with his right hand, and gripped the wrist till he shrieked; then he raised up his mighty left hand, and drave it down on Simon's head by the ear, and all gave way before it, and the murderer fell crushed and dead to earth.

A charge to the guard

Therewith came in the man-at-arms to tell him that the horse was come; but stared wild when he saw the dead man on the ground. But Christopher said: My lad, here hath been one who would have thrust a knife into an unarmed man, wherefore I must needs give him his wages. But now thou hast this to do: take thou this dead man and bind him so fast on the horse thou hast brought that he will not come off till the bindings be undone; and bind withal the head of this other, who was once a great man and an evil, before the slayer of him, so that it also may be fast; then get thee to horse, and lead this beast and its burden till ye are well on the highway to Oakenham, and then let him go and find his way to the gate of the city if God will. And hearken, my lad; seest thou this gold which lieth scattering on the floor here? this was mine, but is no longer, since I have given it away to the dead man just before he lifted his hand against me. Wherefore now I will keep it for thee against thou comest back safe to me in the morning betimes, as I deem thou wilt, if thou wilt behight to St. Julian the helping of some poor body on the road. Go therefore, but send hither the guard; for I am weary now, and would go to sleep without slaying any man else.

So departed the man full of joy, and Christopher gathered his money together again, and so fared to his bed peacefully.

CHAPTER XXXVI. KING CHRISTOPHER COMES TO OAKENHAM

BUT on the morrow the first man who came to the King was the man-at-arms aforesaid; and he told that he had done the King's errand, and ridden a five miles on the road to Oakenham before he had left the horse with his felon load, and that he had found nought stirring all that way when he had passed through their own out-guards, where folk knew him and let him go freely. And, quoth he, it is like enough that this gift to Oakenham, Lord King, has by now come to the gate thereof. Then the King gave that man the gold which he had promised, and he kissed the King's hand and went his ways a happy man.

The errand done

Thereafter sent Christopher for Jack of the Tofts, and told him in few words what had betid, and that Rolf the traitor was dead. Then spake Jack: King and fosterling, never hath so mighty a warrior as thou waged so easy a war for so goodly a kingdom as thou hast done; for surely thy war was ended last night, wherefore will we straight to Oakenham, if so thou wilt. But if it be thy pleasure, I will send a chosen band of riders to wend on the

Jack will send on forerunners

spur thereto, and bid them get ready thy kingly house, and give word to the Barons and the Prelates, and the chiefs of the Knighthood, and the Mayor and the Aldermen, and the Masters of the Crafts, to show themselves of what mind they be towards thee. But I doubt it not that they will deem of thee as thy father come back again and grown young once more.

They ride to Oaken-ham

Now was Christopher eager well-nigh unto weeping to behold his people that he should live amongst, and gladly he yea-said the word of Jack of the Tofts. So were those riders sent forward; and the host was ordered, and Christopher rode amidst it with Goldilind by his side; and the sun was not yet gone down when they came within sight of the gate of Oakenham, and there before the gate and in the fields on either side of it was gathered a very great and goodly throng, and there went forth from it to meet the King the Bishop of Oakenham, and the Abbot of Saint Mary's, and the Priors of the other houses of religion, all fairly clad in broidered copes, with the clerks and the monks dight full solemnly; and they came singing to meet him, and the Bishop blessed him and gave him the hallowed bread, and the King greeted him and craved his prayers. Then came the Burgreve of Oaken-ham, and with him the Barons and the Knights, and they knelt before him, and named him to

The chief men and prelates meet the King

king, and the Burgreve gave him the keys of
the city. Thereafter came the Mayor and the
Aldermen, and the Masters of the Crafts, and
they craved his favour, and warding of his
mighty sword; and all these he greeted kindly
and meekly, rather as a friend than as a great
lord.

Thereafter were the gates opened, and King *They*
Christopher entered, and there was no gain- *enter*
saying, and none spake a word of the traitor *Oaken-*
Rolf. *ham*

But the bells of the minster and of all the
churches rang merrily, and songs were sung
sweetly by fair women gloriously clad; and
whereas King Christopher and Queen Goldilind had lighted down from their horses, and
went afoot through the street, roses and all
kinds of sweet flowers were cast down before
the feet of them all the way from the city gate
to the King's High House of Oakenham.

There then in the great hall of his father's *Triumph*
house stood Christopher the King on the dais, *before*
and Goldilind beside him. And Jack of the *them*
Tofts, and the chiefest of the Captains, and the
Bishop, and the greatest lords of the Barons,
and the doughtiest of the Knights, and the
Mayor and the Aldermen, and the Masters of
the Crafts, sat at the banquet with the King
and his mate; they brake bread together and
drank cups of renown, till the voidee cup was

borne in.   Then at last were the King and the
Queen brought to their chamber with string-
play and songs and all kinds of triumph; and
that first night since he lay in his mother's
womb did Child Christopher fall asleep in the
house which the fathers had builded for him.

CHAPTER XXXVII. OF CHILD CHRISTOPHER'S DEALINGS WITH HIS FRIENDS AND HIS FOLK

IT was in the morning when King Christopher arose, and Goldilind stood before him in the kingly chamber, that he clipped her and kissed her, and said: This is the very chamber whence my father departed when he went to his last battle, and left my mother sickening with the coming birth of me. And never came he back hither, nor did mine eyes behold him ever. Here also lay my mother and gave birth to me, and died of sorrow, and her also I never saw save with eyes that noted nought that I might remember. And my third kinsman was the traitor, that cast me forth of mine heritage, and looked to it that I should wax up as a churl, and lose all hope of high deeds; and at the last he strove to slay me.

Christopher wakens in his own chamber

Therefore, sweet, have I no kindred, and none that are bound to cherish me, and it is for thee to take the place of them, and be unto me both father and mother, and brother and sister, and all kindred.

He hath no kindred

She said: My mother I saw never, and I was but little when my father died; and if I had any kindred thereafter, they loved me not well enough to strike one stroke for me, nay, or to speak a word even, when I was thrust out of my place and delivered over to the hands of pitiless people, and my captivity worsened on me as the years grew. Wherefore to me also art thou in the stead of all kindred and affinity.

Now Christopher took counsel with Jack of the Tofts and the great men of the kingdom, and that same day, the first day of his kingship in Oakenham, was summoned a great mote of the whole folk; and in half a month was it holden, and thereat was Christopher taken to king with none gainsaying.

Began now fair life for the folk of Oakenrealm; for Jack of the Tofts abode about the King in Oakenham; and wise was his counsel, and there was no greed in him, and yet he wotted of greed and guile in others, and warned the King thereof when he saw it, and the tyrants were brought low, and no poor and simple man had need to thieve. As for Christopher, he loved better to give than to take; and the grief and sorrow of folk irked him sorely; it was to him as if he had gotten a wound when he saw so much as one unhappy face in a day; and all folk loved him, and the fame of him went abroad through the lands and the roads of travel, so that many were the wise and valiant folk that left their own land

and came into Oakenrealm to dwell there, because of the good peace and the kindliness that there did abound; so that Oakenrealm became both many-peopled and joyous.

Though Jack of the Tofts abode with the King at Oakenham, his sons went back to the Tofts, and Gilbert was deemed the head man of them: folk gathered to them there, and the wilderness about them became builded in many places, and the Tofts grew into a goodly cheaping town, for those brethren looked to it that all roads in the wood-land should be safe and at peace, so that no chapman need to arm him or his folk; nay, a maiden might go to and fro on the wood-land ways, with a golden girdle about her, without so much as the crumpling of a lap of her gown unless by her own will. *Good peace at the Tofts*

As to David, at first Christopher bade him strongly to abide with him ever, for he loved him much. But David naysaid it, and would go home to the Tofts; and when the King pressed him sore, at last he said: Friend and fellow, I must now tell thee the very sooth, and then shalt thou suffer me to depart, though the sundering be but sorrow to me. For this it is, that I love thy lady and wife more than meet is, and here I find it hard to thole my desire and my grief; but down in the thicket yonder amongst my brethren of the woods, and man and maid, and wife and babe, *Of David*

David will depart

nay, the very deer of the forest, I shall become a man again, and be no more a peevish and grudging fool; and as the years wear, shall sorrow wear, and then, who knows but we may come together again.

David goes over-sea

Then Christopher smiled kindly on him and embraced him, but they spake no more of that matter, but sat talking a while, and then bade each other farewell, and David went his ways to the Tofts. But a few months thereafter, when a son had been born to Christopher, David came to Oakenrealm, but stayed there no longer than to greet the King, and do him to wit that he was boun for over-sea to seek adventure. Many gifts the King gave him, and they sundered in all loving-kindness, and the King said: Farewell, friend, I shall remember thee and thy kindness for ever. But David said: By the roof in Littledale, and by the hearth thereof, thou shalt be ever in my mind.

Comes a man into the hall

Thus they parted for that time; but five and twenty years afterwards, when Child Christopher was in his most might and majesty, and Goldilind was yet alive and lovely, and sons and daughters sat about their board, it was the Yule feast in the King's Hall at Oakenham, and there came a man into the hall that none knew, big of stature, grey-eyed and hollow-cheeked, with red hair grizzled, and worn with the helm; a weaponed man, chieftain-like and warrior-like. And when the serving-men asked him of his name, and whence and whither, he said: I have come from over-seas to look upon the King, and when he seeth me, he will know my name. Then he put them all aside and would not be gainsaid, but strode up the hall to the high-seat, and stood before the King, and said: Hail, little King Christopher! Hail, stout babe of the wood-land! Then the King looked on him and knew him at once, and stood up at once with a glad cry, and came round unto him, and took his arms about him and kissed him, and led him into the high-seat and set him betwixt him and Goldilind, and she also greeted him, and took him by the hand and kissed him; and Jack of the Tofts, now a very old man, but yet hale and stark, who sat on the left hand of the King, leaned toward him and kissed him and blessed him; for lo! it was David of the Tofts.

The King knows him

Spake he now and said: Christopher, this is now a happy day! Said the King: David, whither away hence, and what is thine heart set upon? On the renewal of our youth, said David, and the abiding with thee. By my will no further will I go than this thine house. How sayest thou? As thou dost, said Christopher, that this is indeed a happy day; drink out of my cup now, to our abiding together,

Now will David abide

and the end of sundering till the last cometh.

So they drank together, they two, and were happy amidst the folk of the hall; and at last the King stood up and spake aloud, and did all to wit that this was his friend and fellow of the old days; and he told of his doughty deeds, whereof he had heard many a tale, and treasured them in his heart while they were apart, and he bade men honour him, all such as would be his friends. And all men rejoiced at the coming of this doughty man and the friend of the King.

So there abode David, holden in all honour, and in great love of Child Christopher and Goldilind; and when his father died, his earldom did the King give to David his friend, who never sundered from him again, but was with him in peace and in war, in joy and in sorrow.

CHAPTER XXXVIII. OF MATTERS OF MEADHAM

GOES the tale back now to the time when the kingship of Child Christopher was scarce more than one month old; and tells that as the King sat with his Queen in the cool of his garden on a morning of August, there came to him a swain of service, who did him to wit that an outland lord was come, and would see him and give him a message.

So the King bade bring him into the garden to him straightway; so the man went, and came back again leading in a knight somewhat stricken in years, on whose green surcoat was beaten a golden lion.

He came to those twain and did obeisance to them, but spake, as it seemed, to Goldilind alone: Lady, and Queen of Meadham, said he, it is unto thee, first of all, that mine errand is. Then she spoke and said: Welcome to thee, Sir Castellan of Greenharbour, we shall hear thy words gladly. Said the new-comer: Lady, I am no longer the Burgreve of Greenharbour, but Sir Guisebert, lord of the Green March, and thy true servant and a suitor for thy grace and pardon. I pardon thee not, but thank thee

A messuge

A knight bringeth it

for what thou didst of good to me, said Gold-ilind, and I think that now thine errand shall be friendly. Then turned the Green Knight to the King, and he said: Have I thy leave to speak, Lord King? and he smiled covertly.

But Christopher looked on the face and coat-armour of him, and called him to mind as the man who had stood betwixt him and present death that morning in the porch of the Littledale house; so he looked on him friendly, and said: My leave thou hast, Sir Knight, to speak fully and freely, and that the more as meseemeth I saw thee first when thou hadst weaponed men at thy back, and wert turning their staves away from my breast. Even so it is, Lord King, said the Knight; and to say sooth, I fear thee less for thy kingship, than because I wot well that thou mayst lightly take me up by the small of my back and cast me over thy shoulder if thou have a mind therefor.

Christopher laughed at his word, and bade him sit down upon the green grass and tell his errand straightway; and the Knight tarried not, but spake out: Queen of Meadham, I am a friend and fellow, and in some sort a servant, to Earl Geoffrey, Regent of Meadham, whom thou knowest; and he hath put a word in my mouth which is both short and easy for me to tell. All goes awry in Meadham now, and men are arming against each other, and will presently be warring, but if thou look to it; because all this is for lack of thee. But if thou wilt vouchsafe to come to Meadhamstead, and sit on thy throne for a little while, commanding and forbidding; and if thou wilt appoint one of the lords for thine earl there, and others for thy captains and governors and burgreves and so forth; then if the people see thee and hear thee, the swords will go into their sheaths, and the spears will hang on the wall again, and we shall have peace in Meadham, for all will do thy bidding. Wherefore, Lady and Queen, I beseech thee to come to us, and stave off the riot and ruin. What sayest thou?

He craveth Goldilind for Meadham

Goldilind made answer in a while: Sir Guisebert, true it is that I long to see my people, and to look once more on my father's house, and the place where he was born and died. But how know I but this is some wile of Earl Geoffrey, for he hath not been abounding in trustiness toward us?

The Queen's answer

But Sir Guisebert swore on his salvation that there was no guile therein, and they were undone save Goldilind came unto them. Then spake Christopher: Sir Knight, I am willing to pleasure my Lady, who, as I can see, longeth to behold her own land and people; and also by thy voice and thy face I deem that thou art not lying unto me, and that no harm will befall the Lady; yet will I ask thee right out what

The King would go along with an host

thou and thy lord would think thereof if she come into Meadham accompanied; to wit, if I rode with her, and had five hundreds of good riders at my back, would ye have guesting for so many and such stark lads? The Knight took up the word eagerly, and said: Wilt thou but come, dear lord, and bring a thousand or more, then the surer and the safer it would be for us. Said the King, smiling: Well, it shall be thought on; and meantime be thou merry with us; for indeed I deem of thee, that but for thy helping my life had been cast away that morning in Littledale.

They ride to Meadham

So they made much of the Meadham man for three days, and thereafter they rode into Meadham and to Meadhamstead, Christopher, and Jack of the Tofts, and Goldilind, in all honour and triumph, they and seven hundreds of spears, and never were lords received with such joy and kindness as were they, but it were on the day when Christopher and his entered Oakenham.

Geoffrey giveth his head

The Earl Geoffrey was not amongst them that met them; but whenas they sat at the banquet in the hall, and Goldilind was in the high-seat gloriously clad and with the kingly crown on her head, there came a tall man up to the dais, grey-headed and keen-eyed, and he was unarmed, without so much as a sword by his side, and clad in simple black; and he knelt before Goldilind, and laid his head on her lap, and spake: Lady and Queen, here is my head to do with as thou wilt; for I have been thy dastard, and I crave thy pardon, if so it may be, for I am Geoffrey.

She looked kindly on him, and raised him up; and then she turned to the chief of the serving-men and said: Fetch me a sword with its sheath and its girdle, and see that it be a good blade, and all well-adorned, both sword and sheath and girdle. Even so it was done; and when she had the sword, she bade Sir Geoffrey kneel again before her, and she girt him with the said sword and spake: Sir Geoffrey, all the wrong which thou didest to me, I forgive it thee and forget it; but wherein thou hast done well, I will remember it, for thou hast given me a mighty King to be my man; nay, the mightiest and the loveliest on earth; wherefore I bless thee, and will make thee my Earl to rule all Meadham under me, if so be the folk gainsay it not. Wherefore now let these folk fetch thee seemly garments and array thee, and then come sit amongst us, and eat and drink on this high day; for a happy day it is when once again I sit in my father's house, and see the faces of my folk that loveth me.

She spake loud and clear, so that most folk in the hall heard her; and they rejoiced at her

Goldilind pardons him

And maketh him her Earl again

words, for Sir Geoffrey was no ill ruler, but wise and of great understanding, keen of wit and deft of word, and a mighty warrior withal; only they might not away with it that their Lady and Queen had become as alien to them. So when they heard her speak her will, they shouted for joy of the peace and goodwill that was to be.

There then sat Geoffrey at the banquet; and Christopher smiled on him, and said: See now, lord, if I have not done as thou badest when thou gavest me the treasure of Greenharbour, for I have brought the wolf-heads to thy helping and not to thy scathing. Do thou as much for me, and be thou a good earl to thy Lady and mine, and then shalt thou yet live and die a happy man, and my friend. Or else . . . There shall be no else, Lord King, quoth Geoffrey; all men henceforth shall tell of me as a true man.

So they were blithe and joyous together. But a seven days thence was the Allmen's Mote gathered to the woodside without Mead-hamstead, and thronged it was: and there Goldilind stood up before all the folk and named Sir Geoffrey for Earl to rule the land under her, and none gainsaid it, for they knew him meet thereto. Then she named from the baronage and knighthood such men as she had been truly told were meet thereto to all the offices of the kingdom, and there was none whom she named but was well-pleasing to the folk; for she had taken counsel beforehand with all the wisest men of all degrees.

As for herself, all loved and worshipped her; and this alone seemed hard unto them, that she must needs go back to Oakenrealm in a few days: but when she heard them murmur thereat, she behight them, that once in every year she would come into Meadham and spend one whole month therein; and, were it possible, ever should that be the month of May. So when they heard that, they all praised her, and were the more content. This custom she kept ever thereafter, and she lay in with her second son in the city of Meadhamstead, so that he was born therein; and she named him to be King after her, to the great joy of that folk; and he grew up strong and well-liking, and came to the kingship while his mother was yet alive, and was a good man and well-beloved of his folk.

Goldilind will come off to Meadham

Before she turned back with her man, she let seek out Aloyse, and when she came before her, gave her gifts and bade her come back with her to Oakenham and serve her there if she would: and the damsel was glad, for there in Meadhamstead was she poor and not well seen to, whereas it was rumoured of her that she had been one of the jailers of Goldilind.

Of Aloyse

*Of the
Baron of
Brimside*

When they came back to Oakenham, there they met Gandolf, Baron of Brimside, now whole of his hurts, and the King greeted him kindly, and did well to him all his life; and found him ever a true man.

*The
end of
Chris-
topher*

Good thenceforward was the life of Child Christopher and Goldilind: whiles indeed they happed on unpeace or other trouble; but never did fair love and good worship depart from them, either of each unto each, or of the whole folk unto them twain.

To no man did Christopher mete out worse than his deserts, nay, to most far better he meted: no man he feared, nor hated any save the tormentors of poor folk; and but a little while abided his hatred of those, for it cut short their lives, so that they were speedily done with and forgotten. And when he died a very old man but one year after Goldilind his dear, no king that ever lived was so bewailed by his folk as was Child Christopher.

HERE ENDS THE STORY OF CHILD
CHRISTOPHER AND GOLDILIND
THE FAIR; MADE BY WILLIAM
MORRIS, AND PRINTED AND SOLD
BY HIM AT THE KELMSCOTT PRESS,
UPPER MALL, HAMMERSMITH IN
THE COUNTY OF MIDDLESEX.
FINISHED THE XXVTH DAY OF
JULY, MDCCCXCV.
REPRINTED BY THOMAS B. MOSHER
AT XLV EXCHANGE STREET, PORT-
LAND, MAINE. FINISHED THE
XXIVTH DAY OF NOVEMBER,
MDCCCC.
REPRINTED BY NEWCASTLE PUBLISHING
CO. AT X̄MMMCDXIX SATICOY STREET,
NORTH HOLLYWOOD, CALIFORNIA.
FINISHED THE 1ST DAY OF APRIL,
MCMLXXVII.

NEW RELEASES SPRING 1977

ASTROLOGY AND ITS PRACTICAL APPLICATION,
by Else Parker

This classic work on astro-psychology illustrates the practical value of astrology in everyday life. A.E. Thierens, author of ASTROLOGY AND THE TAROT (also available in a Newcastle edition), called it of "great value for its insights." We are proud to present the first American edition of this splendid book.

P-039-9 212 pages $4.95

VICTOR LINDLAHR's 7-DAY REDUCING DIET

The author of YOU ARE WHAT YOU EAT presents a practical, down-to-earth reducing diet that will get your weight down to where you want it — and keep it there! Here are 201 tasty and imaginative recipes, a helpful question-and-answer section, a calorie counter, and many other important food facts that will put you on the road to eternal slimness. You have nothing to lose but your fat!

H-040-2 128 pages $2.95

PHRA THE PHOENICIAN, by Edwin Lester Arnold

The prospect of immortality has fascinated generations of fantasy writers and readers. Phra the Phoenician is a man who stands astride centuries. Coming to Britain in the time of Caesar, he is struck down in a fiercely-fought battle. But his "death" is only temporary; hundreds of years later he suddenly awakens in an old burial vault, healed and fully alive once again. His journey through the ages is a classic tale of love and adventure. Cover by George Barr.

F-110-7 328 pages $3.95

CHILD CHRISTOPHER AND GOLDILIND THE FAIR,
by William Morris

The author of THE GLITTERING PLAIN and GOLDEN WINGS returns to the Newcastle line with the beautiful story of Oakenrealm, and its stalwart King Christopher and his Queen. William Morris wrote seven fantasies before he died in 1896. We are proud to present the first American edition in 77 years of his least-known novel. With a new introduction by Dr. Richard Mathews, the first Visiting Fellow of the William Morris Centre in England. 4 color cover by Robert Kline.

F-111-5 240 pages $3.45

BORGO PRESS ORIGINALS

UP YOUR ASTEROID! A SCIENCE FICTION FARCE,
by C. Everett Cooper

Things are not well in outer space. The bug-eyed monsters are everywhere, the aliens are running, and UFOs are popping up all over the place. Join us, gentle readers, in this lighthearted romp over the most cherished traditions of the science fiction genre. With a mind-blowing cover by Tony Yamada.

B-206-4 48 pages $1.95

THE BRADBURY CHRONICLES,
by George Edgar Slusser

(The Milford Series: Popular Writers of Today, Vol.4)

The author of ROBERT A. HEINLEIN: STRANGER IN HIS OWN LAND and THE FARTHEST SHORES OF URSULA K. LE GUIN, provides the first comprehensive survey of Bradbury's work, from his first science fiction story, "Pendulum," to his latest collection of short fiction, *Long After Midnight*, published by Knopf in 1976.

B-207-2 64 pages $1.95

JOHN D. MacDONALD AND THE COLORFUL WORLD OF TRAVIS McGEE, by Frank D. Campbell, Jr.

(Milford Series: Popular Writers of Today, Vol. 5)

Beginning in 1964, with publication of *The Deep Blue Good-By*, Travis McGee has rushed his way through sixteen exciting adventures filled with tough action and a bevy of beautiful girls. Frank Campbell covers McGee's entire career, from his first operations on the *Busted Flush*, to his latest saga, *The Dreadful Lemon Sky*.

B-208-0 64 pages $1.95

HARLAN ELLISON: UNREPENTANT HARLEQUIN,
by George Edgar Slusser

(The Milford Series: Popular Writers of Today, Vol. 6)

Harlan Ellison is the most honored science fiction writer in the world today, having won a total of eight Hugo Awards, two Nebulas, three Writers Guild Awards for Most Outstanding Teleplay of the Year, a Jupiter Award, A Mystery Writers of America Edgar Award, and a Nova Award for Most Outstanding Contributor to the Field of Science Fiction. Dr. Slusser examines his rise to fortune, from his first story, "Glowworm," to his most recent hardcover collection, *Deathbird Stories*.

B-209-9 64 pages $1.95

Spring Titles Available April 1, 1977

I. THE GLITTERING PLAIN, by William Morris.
This is the book that reestablished adult fantasy as a distinct category of modern literature. A story of love and immortality, it ranks with the best of Morris's medieval romances. For all lovers of stirring heroic adventure.
F-100-X   174 pages $2.95

II. THE SAGA OF ERIC BRIGHTEYES, by H. Rider Haggard.
Although Haggard is better known for his African romances, this Viking adventure has all of the Master's trademarks: rousing action, bloody battles, unforgettable heroes, romance, and a story that just can't be put down. If you liked *She* and *King Solomon's Mines*, you'll love *Eric*. Illustrated.
F-101-8   304 pages $3.95

III. THE FOOD OF DEATH: FIFTY-ONE TALES, by Lord Dunsany.
(Original title: *Fifty-One Tales*). It's been said that Dunsany, like the writers of ancient Greece, makes his gods human, and his men divine. As any reader will testify, he also writes some of the finest fantasy ever penned. Here's a collection of his best, with a beautiful cover by S. H. Sine.
F-102-6   138 pages $2.95

IV. THE HAUNTED WOMAN, by David Lindsay.
The author of *A Voyage to Arcturus* has written another book as eerie and strange as any fantasy you'll ever read. Put together a ghostly mansion with three rooms that somehow don't exist (or do they?), a piper 1500 years old, reincarnation, love, and supernatural mystery, and you've just begun to explore Lindsay's mystical vision. A superb romance.
F-103-4   178 pages $2.95

V. ALADORE, by Sir Henry Newbolt.
Here's a book that William Morris could have written. Set in a medieval-like world, *Aladore* is the heroic quest of Sir Ywain, who renounces his fiefdom, and sets out to discover his place in the world. How he finds Aithne, the lovely enchantress of Paladore, and all the battles and magic inbetween, is a story that every fantasy lover will want to read. Illustrated.
F-104-2   363 pages $3.95

VI. SHE & ALLAN, by H. Rider Haggard.
The two main characters from *She* and *King Solomon's Mines* finally get it together in this epic sequel of adventure and romance. Ayesha, She-Who-Is-To-Be-Obeyed, calls upon Allan Quatermain to save her from a 2000-year-old mortal enemy. Beautifully illustrated.
F-105-0   302 pages $3.95

VII. GERFALCON, by Leslie Barringer (The Neustrian Cycle, Book One).
In the mythical medieval kingdom of Neustria, Raoul of Ger fight~ ı∩~ his life and fortune in a stirring tale of action and adventure that will leave you riveted to your suit of armor. Don't miss the first book in this thrilling series.
F-106-9   310 pages $3.45

VIII. GOLDEN WINGS, and OTHER STORIES, by William ..orris. With a new afterword by Dr. Richard B. Mathews.
Although Morris wrote these beautiful little tales qı ı~ early in his career, they include many themes present in his later work. "The Hollow Land," "Gerda's Lovers," "Lindenborg Pool," and many other stories are represented. This is fantasy of the first rank.
F-107-7   168 pages $2.95

IX. JORIS OF THE ROCK, by Leslie Barringer (The Neustrian Cycle, Book Two). With a new introduction by Douglas Menville.
This stunning sequel to *Gerfalcon* includes many of the same characters and settings. The infamous outlaw, Joris of the Rock, becomes embroiled in the intrigue surrounding old King Rene, who has a legitimate nephew, Prince Thorismund (the heir), and an illegitimate son, Conrad (who wants the throne). The King dies, Conrad's partisans revolt, and the great battle is joined! With a wraparound cover by George Barr.
F-108-5   318 pages $3.95

X. HEART OF THE WORLD, by H. Rider Haggard.
The great master of fantasy adventure returns to the Newcastle line with the story of an amazing lost city in the Mexican jungles, and a people who have been cut off from civilization for over a thousand years. The Indians are plotting to restore their great empire, and seem on the verge of success when Princess Maya, daughter of the ruler, falls in love with an English explorer. Don't miss the stunning conclusion!
F-109-3   347 pages $3.95

OTHER TITLES OF INTEREST

A. GHOSTS I HAVE MET, by John Kendrick Bangs.
A delightful collection of humourous ghost stories by the author of *A House Boat on the Styx*. Illus.
P-005-4   191 pages $2.45

B. THE BOOK OF DREAMS AND GHOSTS, by Andrew Lang.
The author (with H. Rider Haggard) of *The World's Desire* explores the world of ghostly and occult lore in eighty different tales of the fantastic. A gorgeous cover by George Barr.
P-010-0   301 pages $2.95

C. THE QUEST OF THE GOLDEN STAIRS, by Arthur Edward Waite.
This strange allegorical fantasy tells of the quest of a noble prince of Faerie in search of fame and fortune. Waite is better known for his works on alchemy, magic, and the tarot. For lovers of the arcane.
X-028-3   171 pages $2.95

D. CELTIC MYTH AND LEGEND, by Charles Squire.
Admirers of Evangeline Walton, Katherine Kurtz, Lloyd Alexander, and other fantasy writers will find this massive compendium of Celtic mythology an essential guide to the gods, heroes, giants, and other legendary figures of early Gaelic and British lore. Copiously illustrated.
M-030-5   492 pages $4.95

E. THE ROMANCE OF CHIVALRY, by A. R. Hope-Moncrieff.
Here for the first time in a popularly-priced edition is a comprehensive and authoritative study of chivalry and romantic history, profusely illustrated, with the greatest tales of the knights and heroes of yore retold in clear, exciting prose.
M-038-0   439 pages $4.95

DOCTOR NIKOLA, Master of Occult Mystery, by Guy Boothby $4.95

#1. ENTER DR. NIKOLA! (original title: *A Bid for Fortune*)
A curious chinese token is the key to Nikola's ambitions, and Nikola will have it, whatever the cost. And if Wetherell refuses to sell, perhaps a suitable trade can be arranged: Wetherell's beautiful daughter for the strangely-inscribed stick. Only Richard Hateras can foil the Doctor's nefarious schemes, but Hatteras is being held captive in Port Said, and Nikola has already fled with the girl to the South Seas. Can anyone stop Doctor Nikola?
X-032-1   256 pages $2.95

#2. DR. NIKOLA RETURNS (original title: *Dr. Nikola*)
In his second exciting adventure, Nikola infiltrates a mysterious Chinese sect to gain the secrets of eternal life. With his new assistant, he penetrates the deepest regions of hidden Tibet, where he convinces the princes that he is the newest member of their triumvirate. As the installation begins, the real priest appears, and Nikola is unmasked. The lamas sit in judgment, and their verdict is death!
X-034-8   256 pages $2.95

HEALTH

VICTOR H. LINDLAHR means HEALTHFUL LIVING

i. YOU ARE WHAT YOU EAT.
This classic revelation of diet and nutrition tells you how to balance your meals, where to find vitamins and minerals in natural foods, how to prepare dishes without destroying nutritional content, and much, much more. Includes complete nutritional tables for all fruits and vegetables.
H-004-6   128 pages $2.45

ii. THE LINDLAHR VITAMIN COOKBOOK.
Fresh foods contain all the vitamins and nutrients needed by the human body. The key to preserving these essential constituents lies in the proper preparation of meals and food dishes. Learn how to cook the vitamin way! Complete with vitamin balance charts and recipes.
D-011-9   319 pages $2.95

iii. EAT AND REDUCE!
Diet the Lindlahr way, as America's leading nutritionist outlines a safe and healthy method of getting rid of those exttra pounds. The right kind of reducing diet just can't fail! Includes diet plans and calorie tables.
H-015-1   194 pages $2.45

iv. THE NATURAL WAY TO HEALTH.
Here is Dr. Lindlahr's own story of his research into the natural values of organically grown foods. The secret of good health lies in living a balanced life and eating natural foods. For anyone interested in healthy living.
H-017-8   255 pages $2.95

i-iv. All FOUR books for just $10.00 postpaid!

Other Titles of Interest

v. ROMANY REMEDIES AND RECIPES, by Gipsy Petulengro.
Originally published in this country by E.P. Dutton & Co., Petulengro's book is a classic compilation of Gypsy health foods and medicines, painstakingly discovered by trial-and-error over many centuries of wandering the countrysides of Europe and America. Profusely illustrated.
H-016-X   128 pages $2.25

vi. VIEWPOINT ON NUTRITION, by Dr. Arnold Pike.
Taken from the TV show of the same name, Dr. Pike's book includes interviews with Gaylord Hauser, Dr. Linus Pauling, Eddie Albert, Julie Harris, Sugar Ray Robinson, and many others. Discover the celebrity way of keeping fit! With the Dept. of Agriculture report, "Human Nutrition No.2." An original Newcastle publication.
H-021-6   232 pages $2.95

SELF-ENRICHMENT SERIES

a. FORTUNATE STRANGERS, by Dr. Cornelius Beukenkamp Jr.
This pioneering study of psychology and group therapy has justly been regarded as a classic monograph in its field. "An interesting demonstration — and documentation — of this method in the words of the participants" —*Kirkus Review.* Originally published by Rinehart & Co.
S-000-3   269 pages $2.95

b. LOVE, HATE, FEAR, ANGER, AND THE OTHER LIVELY EMOTIONS, by June Callwood.
A study of human emotions, and how they master, or are mastered by, the individual, *Love* tells us how to use our feelings to our own advantage, and how to maintain a healthy mental outlook on life. Part of this book was accepted in the October 1974 issue of *Reader's Digest.* First published by Doubleday & Co.
S-002-X   170 pages $2.45

c. THE IMPORTANCE OF FEELING INFERIOR, by Marie Beynon Ray
This inspiring book shows how your feelings of inferiority can be used to propel you to greater heights of achievement, and to guide you to a richer, more productive life. Ms. Ray cites many examples from history in demonstrating that self-deprecation is common to us all, and especially to the great achievers in life. Published by arrangement with Harper and Row.
G-006-2   266 pages $2.95

d. THE CONQUEST OF FEAR, by Basil King.
Inspired by the author's incipient blindness, this reprint of the Doubleday edition provides a practical guide to overcoming the fears all of us must face in our everyday lives. A perennial bestseller.
G-009-7   270 pages $2.95

e. MARRIAGE COUNSELING: FACT OR FALLACY? by Dr. Jerold R. Kuhn.
Dr. Kuhn provides a scholarly and timely treatment of a most vital and pressing subject, as drawn from actual case histories in the files of the American Institute of Family Relations. The situations covered range from relatively minor communication problems to more serious difficulties, including incompatibility, sexual disfunction, and money worries. An original Newcastle book.
W-022-4   146 pages $2.95

NOSTALGIA

f. THE ORIGINS OF POPULAR SUPERSTITIONS AND CUSTOMS, by T. Sharper Knowlson.
Knowlson's fascinating account of the follies of human belief includes sections on amulets, charms, divining rods, drinking customs, dreams and omens, crystal gazing, lucky stars, vampires, and more. Complete with index.
W-013-5   242 pages $2.95

g. YOUR HANDWRITING AND WHAT IT MEANS, by William Leslie French.
(originally: *The Psychology of Handwriting*).
An uncomplicated survey of the techniques of handwriting analysis, and how it can be used to reveal hidden character traits in yourself and others. Many signatures of noted personalities included.
G-036-4   228 pages $2.95

h. SECRETS OF STAGE HYPNOTISM, by Professor Leonidas.
The good Professor provides a charming look at the days when hypnotism was a fascinating and mystifying part of stage entertainment. Illustrated with period photographs.
P-029-1   160 pages $2.95

BORGO PRESS ORIGINALS

ROBERT A. HEINLEIN: STRANGER IN HIS OWN LAND, by George Edgar Slusser (The Milford Series: Popular Writers of Today, Vol. 1).
B-201-4   64 pages $1.95

THE BEACH BOYS: SOUTHERN CALIFORNIA PASTORAL, by Bruce Golden (The Woodstock Series: Popular Music of Today, No. 1).
B-202-2   64 pages $1.95

ALISTAIR MacLEAN: THE KEY IS FEAR, by Robert A. Lee (The Milford Series: Popular Writers of Today, Vol. 2).
B-203-0   64 pages $1.95

THE ATTEMPTED ASSASSINATION OF JOHN F. KENNEDY, by Lucas Webb.
B-204-9   48 pages $1.95

THE FARTHEST SHORES OF URSULA K. LE GUIN, by George Edgar Slusser (The Milford Series: Popular Writers of Today, Vol. 3).
B-205-7   64 pages $1.95

To order any of the books listed in this catalog, please fill out this order form, check the number of copies of each title desired, and enclose check or money order for the full amount plus 50c postage and handling. (California residents add 6% sales tax with each order.)

NAME _____

ADDRESS _____

CITY _____ STATE _____ ZIP _____

Please allow four to six weeks for delivery; all prices in this catalog are subject to change without notice.